VALERIE MASSEY GOREE

Meet Me in the Yorkshire Dales

Valerie Massey Goree

Copyright © 2025 Valerie Massey Goree
Winged Publications

All rights reserved. No part of this publication may be reproduced without the prior written permission of the publisher. The only exception is brief quotations in printed reviews. Piracy is illegal. Thank you for respecting the hard work of this author.

This novel is a work of fiction. Names, characters, and events incorporated are a product of the author's imagination. Any resemblance to actual events or persons, living or dead, is purely coincidental.

Scripture quotations, unless otherwise indicated, are taken from the *Holy Bible*, New International Version. Copyright 1973, 1978, 1984, International Bible Society. Used by permission of Zondervan Bible Publishers.

The author has taken liberties with the barn on the Snake Path.

ISBN-13: 978-1-965352-50-2

What Readers Are Saying

Meet Me Where the Windrush Flows

As an avid anglophile, I jumped at the chance to purchase this book. I was already familiar with Ms. Goree's work and knew the story would be unique and the characters relatable. I loved all the description, and easily visualized the tiny Cotswold village, an area I haven't had a chance to visit. The author has obviously done her research on archaeology, and I enjoyed learning about the topic. The male protagonist is a physician, and his tender, yet professional care of his mother is poignant and sweet. There is a bit of mystery and suspense which was fun to follow and try to determine the motive and identity of the villains. I really liked that the main characters were older and had extensive life experiences. Another fantastic book by this author.

*Best-selling author, Linda Shenton Matchett.

The aim of any romance novel should be to let readers fall in love with love and both narratively and stylistically Goree achieves this by creating meaningful conflict, believable characters, and a prevailing sense of emotional honesty that brings her characters to life. Not only are Logan and Grace likable they are easy to cheer for whilst a liberal smattering of misdirection keeps us guessing till the very end!

BookViral review of *Windrush*
"A delightful dalliance into pure escapism..."

"***Forever Under Blue Skies*** made me want to visit Australia. The two mysteries woven into the story kept me turning the pages and the proposal was so romantic, I had to read it twice."

*Amazon Reader Review

CHAPTER 1

Fanning her face with a magazine did little to relieve the stuffiness in the waiting room. The indoor temperature almost matched the early June morning. Roxanne glanced across at the sofa by the window where a blonde with a movie star figure sat, and said, "You'd think lawyers could afford air-conditioning."

"I thought the same thing." The woman gathered her shoulder-length curls into a ponytail and dabbed her nape with a tissue. "Did you by any chance receive a letter demanding your presence here today?"

"I did. It's all a bit mysterious." Roxanne adjusted the patch covering her left eye. "I don't think I'm in trouble, and I know I don't have a wealthy aunt who's named me in her will." She'd fashioned her long hair into a twist secured with a claw clip to keep it off her neck and out of her eyes. The patch seemed to attract stray strands.

"Me neither." The woman pointed to the ornate metal clock on the opposite wall. "Mr. Ogden's running late. I—"

The inner door opened and a tall, elderly woman emerged. "Mr. Ogden will see you now. Please come through."

A sweet but pleasant floral scent surrounded the blonde as she walked past Roxanne and entered the office.

A middle-aged man in a gray suit stood beside an antique oak desk. "I'm Thomas Ogden and I apologize for the warm room and for keeping you waiting. A technician is on his way. My office is much cooler. Please, have a seat." He gestured to the two armchairs and sat in his desk chair. "Would either of you like something to drink? Coffee, water?"

Roxanne and the blonde shook their heads.

"That will be all, Mrs. Edwards."

The tall woman exited through a side door.

The blonde settled on the chair closest to the desk and crossed her legs. The skirt of her maroon dress barely covered her thighs.

For a fleeting moment, Roxanne wished she'd worn something more sophisticated than blue jeans and a coral pink shirt. A trivial thought for such a serious occasion. She perched on the edge of a coffee-colored leather armchair and cleared her throat. Enough dawdling. "Why are we here, Mr. Ogden?"

"Straight to the point. I like that." He smoothed the pages of a file on his desk. "Did you bring identification?"

Roxanne set her passport on the desk and the other woman produced a driver's license.

Ogden opened the passport and looked at Roxanne. "You are Roxanne Ruth Clarke?"

"Yes."

The lawyer picked up the driver's license. "You are Petra Christine Vandiver?"

"I am." Her voice had taken on a silky quality.

"With that important task out of the way, I can tell you why you were invited—"

"Summoned, more like." Roxanne bit her lip as he raised an eyebrow at her. "Sorry."

"Please, no more interruptions. You are here because one of you is the sole heir to your grandfather's estate." He leaned back and folded his arms, a smug expression crossed his oval face.

His statement swirled around the cool room and punched Roxanne in the gut. Seldom at a loss for words, she stammered, "Wh…what?" She stared at Ogden and then at Petra who blinked rapidly and shifted in her chair.

"I know this is a big surprise for both of you, but I will explain." The lawyer pointed to the file.

He sure was taking his sweet time. Roxanne stood and paced to the window. "I don't think I should be here. I'm adopted and was always told I had no blood relatives."

"Same here." Now Petra's voice wobbled as if she was on the verge of tears. "I am curious, though."

"Miss Clarke, please sit down."

She complied with his stern request.

"By the way, why are you wearing a patch?"

Ready to jump up and read the contents of Ogden's folder herself, she glared at him. "You're interested in my physical appearance when my world has just turned upside-down?"

"Please indulge me."

"I had surgery yesterday. A cornea transplant."

"Why?"

As if it were any of his business.

"Please, Mr. Ogden." Petra leaned forward, exposing more cleavage. "Get back to the will. Who is this man and how much…how big is his estate?"

"All in good time. It's apparent neither of you knew you had a grandfather until today. You can wait a few more minutes. Now, Miss Clarke, do you know anything about your birth mother?"

His question knocked the wind out of her frustration. Roxanne swallowed. She'd been devasted by the answers her parents gave her when she'd asked. "No. The adoption was private and closed. I love my parents and they provided a wonderful, secure childhood, but it would be nice to…"

"How about you, Petra?"

She shrugged. "Nope."

"I will now get to the nitty-gritty of your visit."

Roxanne frowned. "Just a minute, Mr. Ogden. If Petra and I share a grandfather, does that make us cousins? If so, wouldn't the eldest inherit?"

"Cool your jets, young lady. It's not that simple."

"Let the man explain." Petra wrung her hands. "Don't you want to know the details?" She uncrossed her legs and then crossed her ankles.

Roxanne glanced at her and could understand her desperation. "Please continue, Mr. Ogden."

"I know your adoptions were closed. However, as adults you can request information about your birth parents from the Central Adoption Registry."

"I didn't know that. Did you, Petra?"

"Nope."

"I have important information, but each of you must sign a permission form before I'll share it with you. Interested?" Ogden's eyebrows rose.

Despite the cool room, adrenalin-heated blood coursed through Roxanne's body. She placed a hand on her chest where she was sure a giant fist squeezed her heart. Did she want to know who her birth parents were? Or learn about her grandfather—apparently a wealthy person?

Petra examined her long, painted fingernails and said, "I am interested. Give me the form to sign."

Before answering the lawyer, Roxanne would love to discuss the matter with her parents who worked at a medical mission in Zimbabwe. Not because she needed their permission, but because she wanted them to be aware before she took this drastic step. Making on-the-spot decisions had never been a problem for her, especially in her career as a nurse practitioner. "Okay, I'll sign the form, too."

Ogden handed out two clipboards, each holding a sheet of paper and a pen. "Read the declaration thoroughly and then sign and date, please."

It didn't take long to do as requested and they returned the forms to him.

"Thank you. I'll sign as the witness and then have copies made for you." He turned to the inner door and called, "Mrs. Edwards."

A couple of seconds later, she entered the office. Ogden handed her the clipboards. "Copies, please."

He set his elbows on the desk and tented his fingers. "Your grandfather is Howard Palmer. Have either of you heard of him?"

The name did flash in Roxanne's memory for a second. "Um, didn't he recently sell his cattle ranch?"

"Correct. He now lives north of San Antonio and because of health issues, wants to locate his grandchild." Ogden held up his hand when Roxanne opened her mouth. He continued, "Mr. Palmer had two children. His daughter died in childbirth thirty-some years ago and Benton, his reprobate son, died in 2014. He led an erratic life. He was an addict, an alcoholic, and a womanizer. My father was Howard's attorney for a long time, and when he retired, I took over the responsibility. We were fully aware of the ins and outs of the Palmer family. Benton had two children we know about." Ogden glanced at Petra and Roxanne in turn. "Here comes the glitch. We recently discovered Benton married one of the women who produced a child; therefore, her offspring is the legitimate heir."

The lawyer's revelation hung in the air like gray smog. Roxanne's father could be Benton Palmer. Absorbing the significant information Ogden shared, she massaged her left temple. "One of us is legitimate and the other isn't? I didn't think people cared about that these days."

"Howard does."

At that crucial moment, Mrs. Edwards entered, handed Ogden the copies, and then left the office.

Petra curled her lip as she looked at Roxanne. "Let me see if I have this straight. She is my half-sister, and either her mother or my mother was married to Benton. But according to your earlier statement, you and Howard don't know which one."

"Correct."

"How do you expect us to find out?" Roxanne's covered eye itched. She resisted the urge to remove the patch and rub it—a big no-no.

Ogden smiled briefly and folded his arms. He seemed to enjoy prolonging the suspense.

"I have a doctor's appointment soon," Petra said. "Please, tell us what we need to do."

The lawyer set two more pieces of paper along

with their copies of the signed forms on the edge of his desk. "Take these, and I'll explain. You'll notice Howard's address and an appointment time for tomorrow. Both of you need to be there. He will give you more information at the meeting."

Roxanne stared at the paper. The words blurred together. She hadn't mastered reading with only one eye yet. Blinking removed the moisture that had gathered in her eye. When her friend Lucas had picked her up that morning, she had no idea she had a grandfather. That she'd meet him. "Do you have any more information for us?"

"I certainly do."

"Good because there are too many holes in your story. My parents told me my adoption was private and closed. I assume Petra's was, too."

She nodded. "Then how did you find us? How do you know we are Benton's kids?"

"My father arranged the adoptions and kept copies of the paperwork."

"Something doesn't ring true." Roxanne frowned. "When did Benton marry? Which one of us was born after that date?"

"And as the mother of the baby, the name of Benton's wife would have been included in the paperwork." Petra's turn to fold her arms. "Ask your father."

Ogden sighed. "I wish I could. He passed away last year." Ogden leaned back in his chair and rocked. "As far as I know, my father only kept the names of the people who adopted you. Benton and his wife had a common-law marriage, and in Texas, they did not have to register with the state. When he was sober, he was a charming man, but when under the influence, he became violent and unpredictable." The lawyer blew out a breath. "I know I'm talking about your father, but most of the time, he wasn't a pleasant man. At least he waited until his children were born before he paid off their mothers."

"Even the woman he married?" Roxanne asked.

"Yes. I guess they'd been exposed to his real personality and decided they were well rid of him." He cleared his throat. "My father found families who wanted to adopt and he took care of the legalities. He took the babies from Benton soon after they were born. Although Dad met the mothers when they signed away their parental rights witnessed by social workers, he didn't make any notes about their appearances."

The profuse amount of information delivered by the lawyer filled Roxanne's brain to capacity. She was ready to storm out of the office before her brain exploded, but she had a couple more questions. "Did Howard meet either woman? How do you know Benton married one of them?"

"Howard did not meet them. When I was helping my father clear out his office, we came across an old file that contained a draft of Benton's will. He named his wife as his sole beneficiary, but in the space for her name, he'd written initials—EAB. Dad recalled Benton telling him he'd supply her name if the marriage lasted." Ogden shrugged. "That gives you a little insight into Benton's personality."

"Wait, wait. You've known the initials of the woman we're looking for all this time and you're just now telling us?" Petra leaned forward as if she was about to confront Ogden physically.

"It was on my list of details to provide you."

"Obviously, the marriage didn't last," Roxanne said.

"Right. He never did tell Dad her full name. A few years after the adoptions, my father wanted to complete Benton's will and called him. Benton said he'd visit the office when he returned from California and added Dad could remove the statement about his wife. They were going to file for divorce but she left the country after giving up her baby. He said nothing about the other woman."

Petra picked up her purse which she'd set on the floor. "I need to leave but I have one last question. If we locate a woman who has those initials but she's deceased, how do we prove she was married to Benton?"

The lawyer stood, stepped around his desk, and shoved his hands into his pockets. "I'm pretty sure she was alive three years ago." He sat on the corner of the desk and swallowed. He ran his fingers under his collar. "One afternoon, my father received a call from a woman who professed to be Benton's wife. He said she didn't know Benton was dead, and then she asked after her baby. Of course, Dad didn't divulge any details."

"Where did she call from? Did you trace the call?" The more Roxanne heard, the more she was sure Ogden deliberately dished out important details one morsel at a time.

"We did. She was in Leeds. That's all we got."

Roxanne's heart beat so hard she was sure the other people in the office could hear it. She rubbed her jaw to ease the tightness as her anger and frustration simmered. "If this woman was legit, she was alive three years ago."

"In England. Was she British?" Petra asked.

"I don't know and Dad didn't elaborate."

Petra rose and slung her purse strap over her shoulder. "Unless *Mr. Palmer* provides more details to help us find this person, I don't see how we can. I've had enough. Goodbye."

"Same here." Roxanne grabbed her crossbody satchel and left the office with her half-sister who climbed into a sleek silver sedan and drove away. Seated outside the building on a bench in the shade, Roxanne slipped on her sunglasses. The smell of freshly mown grass represented a note of normality. She delayed calling Lucas so she could process everything Ogden had shared. Her birth father was Benton Palmer. Her birth mother might have left the country. Her grandfather was wealthy, and she'd meet him the next day.

Such a barrage of information. She prided herself on being independent, able to take care of herself, and seldom needed to ask for advice. However, she had to contact her folks. A phone call was impractical as they had to drive forty miles over rugged dirt roads to the nearest phone. She'd have to email them and hope they had a reliable Wi-Fi connection.

The results of the meeting with Howard Palmer scheduled for the next day would determine her future actions. Identifying her birth mother would be no easy task, maybe even impossible. Should she even try?

Leaning back, she drew in a deep breath. It would take more than a few minutes to analyze the data received. She called Lucas and told him she was ready. Unable to drive for a couple of weeks was more inconvenient than the surgery. Avery, her best friend, was supposed to be her temporary chauffeur, but she had to go out of town and left the day before the surgery. Lucas, Avery's twin brother, volunteered to take her place. All of Roxanne's siblings were unavailable, too. Her estranged sister, Dana, lived in Nevada, two of her brothers, Ramon and Neil, were doing their residency, one in Illinois and the other in Colorado, and Adam, the eldest, worked on an oil rig in the Gulf of Mexico.

So far, Lucas had been a conscientious substitute driver. However, whenever Roxanne spent time with him, she was reminded of their tumultuous relationship that ended two years ago. She thought she'd erased him from her heart, but his broad shoulders, lop-sided smile, and the warmest shade of brown eyes she'd ever seen still had the power to weaken her knees.

CHAPTER 2

Taking care of Roxanne before and after her eye surgery had been the highlight of Lucas's week. He knew she didn't like to depend on other people, so when Avery had an appointment in Houston, he jumped at the chance to take her place.

Roxanne approached his pickup. At only five feet tall, she used the running-board step to climb in. Her scowl and stiff body language told him the meeting had not been a total success. He knew better than to address the topic and waited for her to speak while he eased into traffic on Broadway Road.

"That was the most interesting yet confusing meeting I've ever been in." She adjusted her sunglasses. "I found out who my birth father is, and my grandfather, my real grandfather. He wants to meet tomorrow. Will you be able to take me? He lives north of Boerne."

During the many years he'd known her, she'd never once expressed an interest in finding her birth parents, but on the other hand, she hadn't shared much with him since their break up. "That's interesting. Are you excited?"

"Numb, more like it. Will you come with me?"

"Of course. I'm at your service. What time?"

"Ten o'clock."

In a voice filled with emotion, she relayed details about the strange condition in the will, including particulars about her adoption and her birth father.

"You have to discover which child is legitimate? How are you supposed to do that?"

"I asked the same question. Maybe Howard Palmer, my…grandfather, will provide clues tomorrow." She placed a sheet of paper on the console. "Here's his address."

"Thanks." Lucas stopped at a red light. "What does it feel like to be suddenly confronted with this knowledge?"

"I'm confused, shocked. I need time to evaluate what Ogden told us. Given the names of my blood kin is one thing. Locating a woman who might be in another country is a different game." She folded her arms and stared straight ahead.

Grateful she'd trusted him with the information but aware she must be emotionally exhausted, Lucas changed the subject. "It's close to noon. Do you want to go straight home, or can I take you out to lunch?"

"Can we get takeaway, please? I don't feel like being sociable or tolerating glances at my eye patch."

"Sure. How's your eye? Any pain?"

"Not much. It's itchy and uncomfortable."

She'd want no sympathy. "Does the patch affect your vision?"

"Other than turning my head to see anything to my left, no problem so far."

"Will barbecue be all right for lunch?"

Frowning at him, she nodded. "But no potato salad."

Ahh. Still limiting the carbs. In his estimation, she needn't worry about counting calories. However, during the time they'd dated, she told him about being teased in elementary school when she'd been a little pudgy—her word. The nickname "Boxy Roxy" followed her until middle school when she'd taken up gymnastics. The distress in her voice when she'd told him had caused his heart to sink. Recalling the moment had the same effect. His hold on the steering wheel tightened. She could avoid any food she wanted to.

At the next corner, Lucas turned and had to brake suddenly when a shaggy, mid-sized dog ran out in front of him. "Hey, mutt. Watch where you're going." The dog scurried across the road.

"Lucas, you have to stop. Please." Roxanne had her hand on the door handle.

"Why? What are you going to do?"

"Catch him. See if he has a collar."

Lucas parked and she was out of the truck in seconds. He followed and held her back before she crossed the road.

A young boy carrying a leash hurried down the sidewalk and called, "Rusty. Come here, Rusty." He dodged vehicles as he ran after the dog. The pooch stopped and sat while the boy hooked the leash to his collar.

Roxanne blew out a breath. "I'm so glad he's not a stray."

"Me too." Lucas noted her hands clasped together and her neck straining as her gaze followed the boy with the dog. "Your folks always had dogs."

"Yup. One day when I live in a house and my work schedule isn't so hectic, I want two dogs—one big and one small. And I'll get them for the animal shelter."

Of course, she would. She had a soft heart.

He opened the truck door for her.

"You don't have to do that, you know. I'm perfectly capable—"

"I know. Hush, and get in." Her mouth gaped, her eyebrows rose, and she glared at him, but climbed into the pickup.

He chuckled and after buckling his seatbelt, dared to look at her.

She grinned, then laughed. "What's got into you, Mr. Dupree? You've turned into Mr. Bossy."

"Only when necessary."

"I'll remember that."

Encouraged by her playful reaction, he drove down the street and parked in front of a restaurant known for its delicious barbecue. He understood her comments perfectly. He was not known for being decisive. In fact, that was one reason she broke up with him. In retrospect, he realized a while ago that she found his swaying in the breeze while making decisions to be wishy-washy. Whereas, he thought he was being accommodating to her and Avery by not always taking control.

His time with her now as a captive audience was precious and he wanted to prove to her first that he still loved her, and second that he could make decisions when it counted. He handed the food to Roxanne. "The smaller sack is yours." The spicey aromas from their meals filled the car. He'd ordered extra barbecue sauce for her.

She opened the bag and noted the container of sauce. "You remembered. Thank you."

Her sincere words warmed his heart. "We can't deprive the patient, now. Can we?"

He drove to her apartment complex and walked with her to her door where he lingered, but she didn't invite him in. Unperturbed, he said, "I'll pick you up tomorrow at nine fifteen."

"Thanks, Lucas." She even managed a smile.

On the way home, he mentally reviewed the list of decision-making cues he'd made before he picked up Roxy that morning. The therapy sessions he'd had to help him overcome his indecisiveness offered many avenues for him to try. One was to write down the decisions he knew he'd make that day. So far, he'd even surpassed his expectations. Each one had panned out and he welcomed the sense of accomplishment. He'd made great strides with people in other areas of his life, but being in Roxy's company always threw him off kilter—except when he opened the truck door for her. Today's minor successes went a long way to boost his confidence.

The therapy had been Avery's idea. And as usual, she'd been right. Lucas always believed he lived in her shadow, but he acknowledged why he felt that way during his sessions with Dr. Demetrius Baxter. It was easier to follow her decisions and that way he didn't have to make any and face failure or be ridiculed for being wrong. Memories of their stern father berating and criticizing him for making stupid decisions were never far from his mind. He'd never learned how to please the man.

The one area he was not sorry to have followed Avery's example was his choice of career. They both earned degrees in linguistics and were completing work for their PhDs. He loved the study of languages and dialects, and he had even bested her in a few courses.

Still reveling in his success with Roxanne, he carried his lunch into his condo and sat at his dining table. He cut a slice of brisket and slathered sauce over it. She was right to ask for an extra serving of the tangy concoction. He savored the bite and hoped she enjoyed her meal, too.

He and Avery lived next door to Roxanne and her family throughout junior and high school. She was a few years younger, but fit right in with them. She knew from a young age that she wanted to be a nurse. He'd fantasized about becoming a nurse too, until Roxanne's younger brother, Neil, fell out of a tree and broke his forearm. The splintered bones poked out of his skin. The sight didn't faze her. She yelled for their mother, held Neil's other hand, and stroked his forehead, speaking in a calm tone.

Meanwhile, Lucas couldn't look at the kid's arm, let alone stand anywhere near him. He shook his head as he recalled his slinking away across the lawn and back to his house. No medical career in his future.

Roxanne studied hard through nursing school and eventually earned her nurse practitioner qualifications. She worked at Raglan Clinic which specialized in helping children with special needs and their families. Lucas admired her all the more for her dedication to her patients. She balked at having to take time off for her eye to heal, but she knew she had to. A previous surgery resulted in an infection, and the cornea transplant was the only option for Roxy to save her eye.

Relying on Lucas to drive her places was a situation Roxanne found difficult to tolerate initially. On Friday, the day of her surgery, she barely spoke to him. However, on Sunday, she asked him to take her to church. He didn't realize she was still a member of the denomination her family had attended.

When they'd first started dating, he'd gone with her a few times. After she'd answered his many questions, he was surprised she felt comfortable there. The board of governors for congregations in Texas granted the pastors of individual churches leeway to conduct services as they saw fit, as long as they adhered to the basic tenets of the group. The pastor of Roxanne's church ran the show with a firm hand. He didn't tolerate criticism of his sermons—he stated they were always based on Scripture and challenged anyone to disprove his statement. The pastor seemed to have a long list of don'ts that left little room to rejoice in being a Christian.

Another unusual rule Lucas found almost unbelievable was congregation members were taught that much of the Bible was not to be taken literally. The pastor explained the original texts were written in Hebrew, Aramaic, or Greek, and unless a person knew those languages, he or she couldn't rely on the modern translations to be accurate. Naturally, he had studied those languages, and he determined which parts of the Bible were literal. Nothing Lucas knew about the church seemed to gel with Roxanne's need to be in control and to make decisions for herself.

At the time, Avery had counseled Lucas to leave Roxanne and her beliefs alone. As obstinate as Roxanne was, any interference on his part would only make her dig in her heels. She had to make changes when she was ready.

During the recent Sunday visit, Lucas was surprised to see the same pastor who had been there when they dated. He had paid close attention to Roxanne's demeanor. She wasn't as mesmerized with the service as he remembered she'd been when he accompanied her years ago. Was this a crack in her defenses? He'd have to watch for opportunities to discuss studying Scripture for herself without being told what to believe.

His phone buzzed with a text alert, which terminated his reminiscing. Hoping it might be Roxy, he grabbed the phone off the table. Not Roxy, but Nadine. He hadn't communicated with her in months. Avery and Lucas knew Dr. Nadine Jones from Rice University. While they conducted their research in Yorkshire last year, they attended her lecture at the University of York. She had been lecturing at major universities in the UK, presenting her unique take on language and culture.

When she returned to Texas, she'd offered to read the work they'd done on their proposals so far and offer advice. Avery didn't take her up on the offer but Lucas did. Nadine made suggestions and asked questions which prompted him to take his research in a different direction. He met with her several times, and although he appreciated her advice, he could tell she wanted more than an academic relationship. He gradually decreased the frequency of the meetings but eventually had to tell her he'd given his heart to someone already.

He reread her words.

> *Hey, Lucas. I'll be in San Antonio next week. Can I meet with you and Avery?*

Interesting. He'd reply after he checked with his sister.

Later that evening, when he was tired of research, he switched gears and checked out Howard Palmer online. There were plenty of accolades for his cattle ranching success and contributions to charitable organizations. With no son to inherit, he sold his ranch and moved to Boerne. Lucas hoped he could meet the man, too.

The next morning, armed with his trusty list of possible decisions he'd have to make, Lucas drove to Roxanne's apartment.

She waited out front and climbed into his pickup. "Well, here goes nothing."

"The old man might surprise you. Surely, he has information to help in your search."

"I hope so."

Roxanne wore an emerald green patch that matched her T-shirt. The color emphasized the burgundy highlights in her long, dark hair which hung loose and cascaded halfway down her back. Lucas drew in a deep breath. He'd been in love with her since high school and prayed she'd give him a second chance.

The drive to the Palmer residence took thirty-five minutes. The metal security gate stood open, and as Lucas negotiated the twists and turns of the paved driveway, Roxanne patted his knee.

"A few years ago I thought about finding my birth parents and contemplated taking a DNA test."

"Why didn't you?"

"I'm content to be John and Verna's daughter, and sibling to Dana and the three trouble-makers."

"All that might change after this meeting."

"By the way, I emailed my folks last night. It might be a while before they can respond." She sighed and looked straight ahead.

Lucas parked in the circular driveway. Roxanne was out of the car and stepped onto the vast wraparound porch before he opened his door. She certainly never had an issue with decisions. She knew exactly what she wanted and sometimes walked over people to get her way. Not everyone appreciated that quality the way he did.

A man with bushy gray hair and wearing blue jeans, cowboy boots, and a western shirt, greeted them at the double oak doors. Thumbs tucked into the wide belt, he smiled. "Howdy. I'm Mr. Palmer's foreman, Tyler Hudson."

"I'm Roxanne and this is my friend, Lucas." She touched her eye patch. "Because of my recent surgery, I can't drive right now."

Petra arrived and joined them on the porch.

Tyler invited them into the grand foyer and stopped at a closed door. "You can wait here, Lucas."

"I want to accompany Roxy. If you don't mind."

She frowned again at him and he grinned.

Footsteps on the wooden floor sounded behind him. He and Roxanne turned in time to see a slim, silver-haired woman walk across the foyer.

Lucas and the two granddaughters were ushered into a large wood-paneled room. Built-in shelves crammed with books lined two walls. The earthy smell of old leather and paper filled the room. A maroon carpet covered the oak floors.

Howard Palmer sat behind a large mahogany desk, arms folded across his sizable paunch.

As Lucas drew nearer, he noted the wrinkles on the man's face reminded him of a map with roads crisscrossing each other. Sparse tufts of white hair covered his scalp, the collar of his faded blue shirt, and his tanned forearms. His pale blue eyes were almost hidden by the folds of skin on his eyelids. If Lucas had passed him in the street, he would have thought the man was strapped for cash. When Howard spoke, Lucas expected a quavering voice, but he sounded like a football coach addressing his team.

"Come closer. Let me take a gander. Tyler,

introduce them, please."

The foreman did as requested and included the reason for Lucas's presence.

Palmer stood and circled the desk, his back as straight as a soldier at attention, and shook hands with the three guests. Keeping hold of Roxanne's, he said, "Eye surgery. I can see the need for a driver, but do you trust him to be privy to our family secrets?"

"I do. He's an old friend."

Palmer gestured to armchairs surrounding a coffee table and sat in the chair with worn upholstery, probably his favorite. "I don't have much time, but I want to know what type of eye surgery you had, Roxanne."

She squared her shoulders, certainly not intimidated by the larger-than-life man. Petra, on the other hand, seemed to shrink in the chair when Palmer looked at her, completely the opposite reaction to what Lucas expected when he'd first seen her. Dressed in a white suit with navy edging, high-heeled navy shoes that matched her purse, and her blonde hair bouncing on her shoulders when she walked, she exuded confidence as she stepped into the house.

"I had a partial cornea transplant. Several years ago I suffered an eye injury that became infected. The infection didn't respond to antibiotics and it scarred my cornea. My vision was affected, and I was put on the waiting list for a transplant."

"Does it hurt?" Petra asked.

"Not much. The swelling will go down in a few days, but the worst part is I have to stay off work for several weeks—"

"And she can't drive until the surgeon clears her." Lucas glanced sideways at Roxanne.

She harrumphed. "Yeah, my vision will be blurry for a while, but special contacts might help."

"All very interesting. Now, down to business. As you recall, my will is very specific. Most of my estate will go to whichever child can prove her mother married my son." He rubbed his balding head. "Otherwise, it will all go to my favorite charity. My worthless nephew won't get a cent."

CHAPTER 3

For a brief second, a smug expression crossed Howard's face. Roxanne also noted he glanced at Tyler as if they conspired together.

Tossing her blonde curls over her shoulder, Petra said, "Before this meeting progresses any further, I need answers, please. First of all, will you provide clues to help us find your son's wife?" She wiped her palms on the arms of the chair. "And what is the size of your estate? Is it worth the time and effort we'll have to expend? I don't know how Roxanne feels, but I'm content with my adoptive parents. I could care less about my birth parents."

The old man raised his chin and worked his jaw muscles, clearly not happy with the questions, but he replied, "I do have information to give you that might lead to finding your mother. As to my estate… I owned the third-largest cattle ranch in Texas for many years. I was successful because I diversified. Grew our feed. Rented out facilities. Tyler's wife ran a successful wedding venue business. When I sold up, I purchased this house and ten acres and had enough left to—" He coughed, grimaced, and placed his hand over his heart.

Roxanne rose and approached him. "Mr. Palmer, I'm a nurse. What's wrong." She knelt beside him and felt his pulse which was slightly elevated.

Tyler searched the desk drawers. "Where are your pills?" He finally found them under a folder on the desk and gave Howard one which he placed in his mouth.

"Are you going to call for an ambulance?" Lucas asked.

"Not necessary if the nitroglycerin pills do their job." Roxanne kept her fingers on his pulse. "When was he diagnosed with angina?"

"Three, four years ago. The stress of this meeting could have brought on an episode."

"I think you should contact his physician."

"I usually do."

Howard's color slowly returned to normal. He asked Tyler for a glass of water, and after sipping half the contents of the glass, he addressed his guests. "I'm sorry you had to witness that. Thank you, Roxanne." He waved a hand at his desk. "Tyler, please give me the yellow folder." Once in his hand, he opened it and removed two sheets of paper. "This one's for you, Petra, and Roxanne, take this one."

The paper listed names, places, and dates. Roxanne

returned to her seat, looked at Howard, and jabbed at the paper. "How will this help us?"

"I compiled these details about events I know Benton attended and the names of some of his friends who can confirm my information." Howard snorted. "I even included my nephew on the list. He probably won't be able to help as he and Benton weren't close. I know my son was a scoundrel. He had many women and may have more children than you two."

Tyler moved closer to Howard. "You need to rest, sir."

"I will, in a minute. I'm almost through. Give them the envelopes."

The foreman took two sealed envelopes from the desk. He handed one to Petra and one to Roxanne.

The old man nodded. "Each envelope contains a letter which will answer your questions. Open them after you leave the room, please." He rested his head on the back of the chair. "One more thing. When we moved from the ranch house where I'd lived for sixty years, I found an old chest filled with Benton's belongings. I didn't go through it but you might find something of interest in there. Tyler will show you where the chest is. And Tyler, give them your phone number so they can text you about any progress they make in locating the right woman. And, here, catch." He tossed Tyler a key.

Tyler motioned for the three guests to follow him. He escorted them to the back of the house and opened a door to a small room. "In case you're wondering, Benton had a bedroom at the ranch and stayed there between exploits. Howard may not have approved of his son's activities, but he didn't disown him. It's in here." He entered the room first and unlocked the chest. "Take as much time as you need. I have your phone numbers and will text you later."

"Have you looked in the chest?" Roxanne stuffed Howard's letter into the back pocket of her slacks.

"No. Howard only gave me the key right now." He left the room, his boots marking his progress down the hall.

She grabbed Lucas's arm. "Can you stay a while longer?" She had to admit his presence acted like a shot of adrenaline. Normally, when treating charming or cantankerous old men, she gave the orders. Following Grandfather's strange directions was a new experience for her.

"Of course."

"Well, I can't stay long. Let's start looking." Petra opened the honey-colored wooden chest and the hinges squeaked. A musty odor emanated.

Lucas removed the wooden tray on top and set it on the round table close to Roxanne.

She sat and examined the contents. Books, a container of toy army men, the wheels from a skateboard, and a pink woolen scarf wrapped in tissue paper.

The scarf interested her. Someone cared enough to

protect it. Mingled with the musty aroma was a delicate floral scent. Could the scarf have belonged to one of the women? She searched for a label but found none. Moths had made several holes along one edge. On the off-chance it did belong to her mother, Roxanne set it aside.

Meanwhile, Petra rummaged through the contents of the chest. She dumped pieces of men's clothing on the carpet. "I don't see how any of this can help us. I'm leaving." She placed a business card beside Roxanne. "Please, contact me if you find anything significant. I think the old man is stringing us along. However, my fiancé is a lawyer. I'll ask for his opinion."

Roxanne nodded, not sure she would share anything she found. Petra needed to put in the time and effort, too.

A tentative knock sounded and the silver-haired woman she'd seen briefly in the foyer poked her head around the door. "I hope I'm not intruding but I have some information that might help your search."

"Please, come in." Roxanne gestured to another chair. "Join me."

"Thank you. I'm Carol Newcombe, Howard's sister-in-law. My husband passed away years ago, and when my sister had a stroke, I came here to help her. After she died, Howard graciously invited me to stay."

Ah. So the "worthless nephew" wasn't her son. Roxanne introduced herself and Lucas. "I assume you know why we're here. Howard's other grandchild left seconds before you entered."

"Yes, she passed me in the hall. Not to worry. I think my information is for you, Roxanne."

Her heart rate increased. "You...you knew my mother?"

"Maybe. Benton didn't often bring his women to the ranch. I remember one time he arrived with a lovely young English girl. You have similar color hair, but hers wasn't as dark. Her name was Emily Anne and she had an unusual accent."

"Emily Anne. Are you sure?" The name corresponded with the initials in the draft of Benton's will.

"Oh, yes. They stayed for a weekend while Howard was at a cattle auction in Fort Worth. Benton treated Emily Anne like a porcelain doll. She didn't wear a wedding ring, but if Benton was going to marry anyone, I wouldn't be surprised if it was her." Carol hung her head for a second. "I'm not proud of what I did. I wanted to learn more about Emily Anne so I snuck into their bedroom and saw a book of poetry on the bedside table. I recognized Benton's handwriting. On the flyleaf, he'd written, 'To my darling Emily Anne.' I knew then she was special to Benton. I didn't have time to check anything else." She swiped a tear off her wrinkled cheek. "For once, he was sober, and I don't think he was using. He'd been such a sweet kid, and I saw a smidge of that personality again. I cried when they left."

"When was this?"

"Soon after my sister passed away. I'd say late 1995."

Lucas had quietly moved to stand beside Roxanne. He placed a hand on her shoulder. "You were born the next year."

She nodded, her throat too full to utter a word.

In the distance, a voice called, "Carol. We need to leave."

"Tyler's taking me to the airport. I usually spend the summers with my daughter in California." She pushed back her chair. "One last thing. I mentioned Emily Anne had a strong accent and sometimes used unusual words. She'd say 'ta-ra' for goodbye and 'summat' for something." Carol walked toward the door.

"Wait. Did you ever see her again?"

"No, and I didn't know anything about the babies. I would have…" She wrung her hands. "Howard and Tyler are waiting. I hope I've helped. Ta-ra."

Lucas knelt beside the chest. "I have an idea about Emily Anne's accent, but I'll wait to share my thoughts with Avery."

"No fair, Lucas. Tell me, please." Roxanne stared at him in an effort to intimidate him.

He ignored her and discarded a sweater and a pair of jeans from the trunk. "I suppose it won't hurt. And she can correct me if I'm wrong. Some people from Yorkshire say ta-ra."

"Do people from Yorkshire have unusual accents?"

"Avery and I thought so."

She closed her eyes. Within the space of twenty-four hours, she'd gone from being content with her adoptive family to fantasizing about a mother with an English accent. No, a Yorkshire accent. Roxanne opened her eyes and smiled. As if she knew the difference.

Maybe to prolong the search or to give herself time to process the significance of the moment, she asked, "Tell me, why are you two Texans studying accents in Yorkshire? Haven't they done that themselves?"

"Of course they have. My focus is comparing the development of dialects in Yorkshire, the largest county in England, with the evolution of the Appalachian English dialect."

"Why that…dialect?"

"For two reasons. It's derived from a combination of German, English, Scottish, and Irish groups that gradually moved south from the original colonies in the early eighteenth century. Secondly, it is one of the oldest dialects in our country and the most intact."

"Because the populations tended to remain in their communities and not move around."

"Exactly."

"Very investing. I'd like to hear more about your comparisons."

"And I'd love to share my studies with you."

The conversation was swiftly heading in a

direction she wasn't ready to travel. Back to the job before her, Roxanne examined the titles of the books. A few sci-fi novels, an old manual for a 1980 Mustang, a dictionary, and a journal, which she opened immediately. However, many pages had been ripped out, and there was no writing in it at all. She shook the other books, and no interesting bits of paper floated out. "Rats. Nothing is exciting in the books."

Lucas yanked out a pair of blue jeans and they landed with a thud on the floor. "That might be exciting." Shoving the fabric aside, he located a well-used book. He picked it up and turned it over. "Here, Roxy. This might interest you." He slid the book across the table to her.

She read the title and frowned. A volume of poetry by Sylvia Plath. It seemed incongruent with Benton's personality. Or at least what she knew of him. On the other hand, it could be the book Carol mentioned. Fingers shaking, Roxanne opened the book, but no inscription was inside. The page had been removed. Too much to hope for.

Sighing, she thumbed through the poems and found one with a very unusual title— "You're". The verses were heavily underlined. She only understood the title after reading the short poem twice. It was about a pregnant woman. The book probably belonged to Emily Anne who might be her mother. Was she pregnant at the time and identified with the poet? Roxanne set the book with the scarf and asked Lucas,

"Have you found anything?"

"Maybe. Petra shouldn't have given up so quickly. This was at the bottom of the chest." Holding up a black satin bag closed with a drawstring, he stepped to the table and opened the bag. Cautiously inserting his fingers, he withdrew a small box covered in green velvet.

"That looks interesting."

Lucas opened the box. A brooch the size of a silver dollar rested on a bed of beige satin. The disc depicted a white flower edged in green and gold. He handed it to her.

"This is exquisite. It must be significant."

"Do you think Howard would know?"

She shrugged and set the brooch back into the box. "I don't think so. He never met either woman. According to Carol, Benton wasn't in the habit of taking his women to the ranch. I wish she hadn't left because I have so many questions."

"That's not all." He tipped the bag and a locket fell out.

Roxanne picked up the delicate, silver circle, about two inches high, and pried it open while Lucas peered over her shoulder. For a moment, his warm breath tickled her neck, and... Then he took the locket from her fingers and she blinked away the memory.

The locket contained a faded headshot of a woman. "Wouldn't a photograph be the perfect clue if it was of my mother?"

He studied the picture. "Hmm. I think I see a resemblance."

Roxanne said, "Ha-ha. Wishful thinking."

"Probably. If we don't have any joy with the information we have so far, we can always wait until Carol returns and ask if she recognizes the woman."

"I suppose."

He returned the brooch and the locket to the bag and handed it to Roxanne. While tossing the discarded clothes into the chest, he asked, "Do you want to take anything else?"

"The book of poetry, the scarf, and of course the jewelry."

He set the tray inside the chest and closed the lid.

Roxanne stood and the envelope fell out of her back pocket. "Oops. I forgot Howard gave us these letters. Let's read mine before we leave."

To my grandchild:

> *All this is as strange for me as I'm sure it is for you. I knew Benton was a womanizer, but I thought he'd be smart enough to prevent any pregnancies. However, I only found out about you two a few months ago. My lawyer, Samuel Ogden—you met his son yesterday—told me just before he retired. He made the arrangements with Benton for the children to be adopted. You two. I was deliberately left out of the loop, as per Benton's request. Naturally, Samuel*

obliged. He paid the women to relinquish their rights to the children and to disappear.

As I explained when I met you today, I will only acknowledge the legitimate child. Unfortunately, Benton did not tell anyone the name of his wife. All I know is, he professed to have a common-law marriage here in Texas. He never said where the child was born. I assume at home. As I said, Samuel handled all the legalities.

I know. I know. Not much to go on. Questioning Samuel's son might help but he was supposed to share all the pertinent details with you yesterday. Tyler and Benton weren't friends, so he probably doesn't have anything to add.

I have nothing else to say except I hope you find out who is my heir before I pass away.

Howard John Palmer

Shoulders sagging, and feet dragging, Roxanne walked to Lucas's truck. The letter didn't provide additional information about the women, and it seemed Howard knew very little. At least Carol supplied them with a few nuggets. Lucas opened the passenger door for her and she climbed in without insinuating she could open her door. When they dated, he'd always opened her door.

Buckling her seatbelt, she gazed out the side window. Avery better take over as her chauffeur because being in such close proximity to Lucas was becoming hazardous to her heart.

Once in the truck, she read the book's back cover blurb. "The author of these poems is American but lived in Yorkshire for a long time. Sylvia Plath."

"It's unfortunate the inscription's been removed."

"Yeah. But I think it is the book Carol saw in Emily Anne's bedroom. I suppose I should let Petra know about the book, the photograph in the locket, and the brooch."

"You can take a photo of the pin, make a copy of the picture, and give her the name of the poet."

"That's a good idea. I'll make copies at home and email them to her." As Lucas made his way back to San Antonio, she examined the brooch and looked up its description online. "Hey, this flower is a symbol of Yorkshire, the white rose of York. That's another point in favor of England." She giggled. "Want to make a trip across the pond?"

"With you? Certainly."

Roxanne slipped the jewelry pouch into her pocket and gazed out the side window. She hadn't been in Lucas's company much over the past year and noticed several changes in his behavior. He was much more assertive, but not in a negative way, and he hadn't hesitated once since being her driver. When Avery returned, she'd have to ask her what her brother was up to.

He stopped outside her apartment building and said, "I know you're going to share the information you found with Petra, but let her discover the Yorkshire connection. I have an inkling Howard Palmer is a very wealthy man. You deserve to be his heir. I know many people will benefit from your newfound wealth."

"Thanks, Lucas. I haven't let myself think about the financial aspect, but it certainly opens up a world of opportunities." She removed her sunglasses. "Thanks for coming with me today. I mean for being with me in my audience with Grandfather. He was a bit intimidating."

"You intimidated? I don't believe it. All in a day's work. I'll send my bill at the end of the month."

She slapped his shoulder. "You are so silly sometimes." *I don't know what's going on with you, Mr. Dupree, but I like the changes you're making.*

The next day, Lucas drove her to her follow-up appointment with the surgeon. Her eye was healing but she needed to keep it covered with a patch or a plastic shield. The doctor repeated the restrictions which she balked at, but she didn't want to lose her vision and promised to follow the precautions. She could tolerate two more days of being chauffeured.

The most annoying aspect of the recovery was only having the use of one eye. She found herself moving her head frequently to see things to her left. Even without a patch, sight from her left eye was blurry at best. Lucas stood as she entered the waiting room, and as they walked to the parking area, she decided to test her new philosophy.

"Hey, Lucas, I need to purchase a few groceries. Can you take me, please?"

"Of course. Which store?"

"It doesn't matter. You choose."

He opened her door and frowned. "Um, I like H-E-B. It's just around the corner."

"That'll be fine. Thanks."

Seated behind the wheel, he ran a hand across his brow before he reversed out of the parking space. When he reached the cross street, he stopped and looked both ways. Twice.

Roxanne didn't notice any vehicles either way. Had Lucas's indecisiveness returned? She turned to ask him a question and… Crunch. Glass shattered. Bang. The side airbag exploded, hitting her shoulder. She gasped and then…darkness.

CHAPTER 4

"Roxanne!" Lucas fumbled with his seatbelt and then leaned toward her. He cradled her head and she scrunched up her eyes. "Roxy, are you all right?"

"What...happened? What's that smell?"

"Your airbag deployed which produced a smokey odor. Are you hurt?"

"My shoulder."

"Be still. I'll call for an—"

Someone knocked on his door and he opened the window.

A woman leaned in. "I've called the cops and an ambulance. Anyone injured?"

"My passenger is. Thanks for calling the authorities. Did you see what happened?

"I did. Took a photo of the car that hit you and captured part of the license plate number. I think he hit you deliberately."

Although not injured, Lucas's heart beat raced as if he'd run ten miles. "Roxy, the ambulance will be here soon. Did the airbag hit your eye?"

"No. I'd turned toward you so the bag hit my shoulder."

He held her hand and she didn't squirm. "I'm so sorry. I didn't see any vehicles coming. "I'll never forgive myself…"

She squeezed his fingers. "That woman said it wasn't your fault."

Minutes later, sirens punctuated the hot, humid air.

"Well, well, well. Some people will do anything to get sympathy." Avery set her hands on her hips as she entered the hospital room.

"Never mind her, Roxy. She's jealous because I went with you to Howard's home." Lucas moved two chairs close to the bed.

"No, I'm not."

Roxanne covered her ears with her hands. "With all this commotion, the staff might throw me out."

"Seriously, Roxy Ruth. When will you be discharged?" Avery placed Roxanne's change of clothes on the bed.

For most of their lives, Avery had asked the questions before Lucas even thought of them. Since she hadn't seen Roxanne for a week, he didn't mind. But being more assertive with his sister was another area he was working on. It had always been easier to go along with her but at thirty, it was time he stopped being her easy-go-lucky twin and started carving out his own path.

"Soon. My ophthalmologist visited an hour ago, and the impact from the airbag didn't affect my eye. The doctor set my dislocated shoulder yesterday when I arrived. So all's good. I'm waiting on paperwork."

"I'll take you home. I'm sure you've had enough of my brother's company. Too bad he has to ride with us."

Lucas smiled. Avery knew he had received therapy for his issues, but she didn't know that his goal was to date Roxy again. He let her statement pass for now because it was probably true. He'd seen more of Roxanne since her surgery than he had in eighteen months. There was no telling what might happen with a possible trip to England on the horizon.

"I'm glad I had my phone with me. Tyler texted and asked if we found anything of interest in the chest. I told him about the locket and photo. I asked after Howard's health, and he reported the man went to his doctor, who said, 'He's doing as well as can be expected.' Standard doctor speak. I also requested he send me Carol's phone number or email so I can send her a copy of the photo. She'll know if the woman is Emily Anne."

"That's a great idea."

Ten minutes later, a nurse delivered the paperwork. After Roxanne dressed, Lucas escorted her to the patient pick-up exit while Avery collected her car from the valet. Ignoring Roxanne's objections, Lucas squeezed into the backseat.

"I'm going to raise the top to keep the wind out of Roxy's eye." Avery engaged the switch and the hardtop opened up and clicked into place.

With his knees under his chin and his head touching the top, he grinned. He wouldn't tolerate such discomfort for anyone but Roxanne. The ride to her apartment was long enough to cause his thigh muscles to cramp. Lucas unfolded his legs and stepped out of the car.

She waited on the sidewalk and when he approached her, she leaned close and whispered, "You didn't have to do that, you know."

"I'd only do it for you."

A hint of a blush tinged her cheeks as Avery and Lucas walked with her to her door.

"Thanks for the ride. I won't invite you in, but can you both come for supper tomorrow?"

"I'd love to, Roxy, and I can examine all the items you and Lucas found in the chest. Do you need anything from the grocery store?"

"If I do, I'll ask my neighbor to take me."

Lucas had met Brenda several times when he and Roxanne—

"Oh, there he is. Hey, Vince." She waved to a blond Adonis with a toothpaste commercial smile who unlocked a door down the hall.

"Rox, how's your eye?"

"Healing, thank you."

Squelching a grain of jealousy, Lucas said, "What time tomorrow? I haggled with my auto insurance for hours and can pick up my rental in the morning. No more scrunching up in my sister's tin can." Even climbing into the front seat was hard on his knees. Avery was only a few inches shorter but never had a problem. Probably years of wrestling in high school and college contributed to his lack of flexibility.

Roxane giggled and opened her door. "How about seven?"

"Perfect." Avery set her arm around Lucas's shoulders. "I'm glad you'll have your own transportation. That means you won't clutter up my beautiful vehicle again."

"I'm excited to show you what we found, and I need to share ideas clamoring for attention in my brain but I don't know which ones to heed." Roxanne removed her eye patch.

"Okay. Glad to help. See ya, Roxy Ruth."

Once behind the wheel, Avery lowered the top of the convertible. "I'm curious about the items you found. Are you convinced the clues point to Yorkshire?" She drove out of the parking lot and headed toward Shavano Park subdivision.

"Yes, and I'm sure you'll agree."

"If so, you know Roxy *will* travel to England. You know how determined she can get."

"Right, and I will accompany her." He folded his arms. Roxanne might have been teasing when she'd asked him, but his reply had been sincere.

"Are you serious?"

"Why not? I can clarify a few points for my dissertation proposal, enjoy cooler temps while helping her."

"Do you mind if I tag along?"

He raised his eyebrows and stared at her. When had she ever asked his permission? "No, but it's not my decision."

Avery tapped the steering wheel. "Going back to Yorkshire will help me with a part of my proposal, too. I want to focus more on dialect differences in rural communities."

"I'm almost through with mine, but Dr. Katherine Kalk from the University of York has been trying to locate a man who has accumulated a lot of information on the strong presence of Old English sounds in the Yorkshire dialect and the impact of the Norse language."

Avery parked outside his condo building. "That sounds interesting. How did it go with Roxy? Did you use the techniques Demetrius suggested?"

"I did and they worked well until she asked to go to a grocery store. She said she didn't mind which one, and I froze. I couldn't remember where H-E-B was and...and that's when the truck hit us."

"But you'd made progress before that, right?" She covered a yawn. "Whew. I'm tired."

"You look pale. Are you feeling okay?"

"Yeah. Have you heard anything from the cops?"

"The vehicle was stolen, so no help there. I hope it was an accident."

"Me too. Roxy doesn't have any enemies. But the eyewitness said the pickup headed right for the passenger door, right?"

Lucas eased his long legs out of her convertible. "Yeah. The only person I can think of is Petra, the other woman in line to be Howard's heir."

"That's a possibility. Do you know anything about her?"

"Only what I observed during the meeting at Howard's home. She seemed eager to know the size of the inheritance, she fidgeted a lot and then left abruptly before we'd searched the chest."

"Hmm. I wonder if she will contact Roxanne."

"Before I go, I need an answer. Can you meet with Nadine this evening? Please come. I don't want to go alone." His neck heated at the thought.

"Oh, brother dear. Do you still get flustered at the mere mention of her name?"

"Stop."

"Okay. Let's meet at the café down the street from my place at six. I don't want a late night."

"I'll text her as soon as I get home."

"Change the subject. How long will it take for your truck to be repaired?"

"Not long. The chassis wasn't damaged."

"Instead of driving a rental, ask Dad to borrow his pickup."

"Nope."

Avery had a good relationship with their father, but Lucas did not. He waved to her and entered his condo. Telling Avery about the accident had brought to mind the flaw in his plan when he'd been with Roxy—dealing with the unexpected. He and Demetrius had reviewed countless scenarios that involved his friends or colleagues, but they had not specifically addressed his interactions with Avery or Roxy. Lucas believed he could handle his sister since he knew her so well and she was acutely aware of his problem. Maybe he should wing it when with Roxy instead of trying to script every encounter.

The meeting with Nadine was interesting. She'd arrived at the restaurant before Lucas. He sat across from her, relieved she didn't stand and hug him.

"What would you like to drink, Lukey?"

He did not like the nickname, but she insisted on using it no matter how much he protested.

The waiter approached their table with a pad and pencil ready.

"Just water, please, and bring a glass for the other guest."

"Still a teetotaler, I see."

"Yeah, except for an occasional margarita. You look well, Nadine." Her bronze skin glowed in the ambient light, and her straightened black hair framed her face.

"You do, too. Ah, here's your sister."

Lucas stood and pulled out a chair for Avery.

She sat and smiled at Nadine. "This is quite the surprise. Are you back in Texas now?"

"I've accepted a full-time position at Rice University. Before the fall semester begins, I want to complete my next book."

The waiter delivered the glasses of water and took their orders.

"I can't stay long and just want dessert. The cheesecake with caramel sauce, and please bring it right away." Nadine set aside the menu and glanced at Lucas. He was sure she winked.

Talk about being flustered. He could hardly see the print on the menu and just ordered the same thing Avery did—chicken fried steak.

While consuming her dessert, Nadine explained the reason for the meeting. "My next book focuses on how accents differ between first-generation Jamaicans in North Yorkshire, specifically Leeds, and those in South Yorkshire, specifically Sheffield, and research how the local dialects influence them. I'd like to discuss my findings with your contacts in Leeds. Will you share their details with me?"

Lucas looked at Avery. As far as he was concerned, Nadine's request shouldn't pose a problem. He waited for his sister's response.

"I'll contact our friends and ask if they will communicate with you. If they agree then we can email you their details. How's that?"

"Good. Thank you." She pushed aside her empty pale. "That was excellent. I appreciate your assistance. You both should be about ready to defend your proposals."

"We are. The concept for your next book sounds exciting. Your Jamaican roots will give you a unique approach." Avery sliced a small piece of steak and popped it into her mouth.

Lucas leaned back and folded his arms. He could relax now. Nadine's request would be easy to fulfill and he wouldn't have to fend off her advances.

CHAPTER 5

At noon the next day, Roxanne called. "Are you coming over for supper tonight?"

"Of course. What can I bring?"

"Avery's bringing a salad. Can you supply the dessert?"

"I know just what to make." The only area where he outshone his sister was in the kitchen. She hated to cook, whereas he considered himself a master chef. Or at least a competent cook.

Lucas was anxious for the evening to go well but decided to build on the confidence gained from previous successes with Roxy and not prepare a script for the possibilities. At some point, he'd have to go cold turkey and adjust to every circumstance.

When working with Demetrius, he'd recalled the moment his ability to make decisions had been shattered. The moment his father shouted the words that were etched into his brain. "Hurry up. How long does a normal kid take to choose between chocolate or vanilla? You're worthless. Why don't you sell your brain since you're not using it? I'm surprised you even know how to breathe." Lucas had walked out of the kitchen empty-handed while Avery carried a bowl of chocolate ice cream.

Shaking off the memory, he settled at his desk and worked on his proposal and a journal article he was writing. Hours later, he gathered the ingredients for his famous Key lime pie, a light, refreshing dessert for a summer meal.

Lucas arrived at Roxanne's apartment before Avery. The hostess welcomed him in with a genuine smile while thumping chords of music played in the background and delicious aromas of chili tickled his tastebuds. He recognized the composition as "Celtic Metal" by the group Lords of Iron. She still liked them, although the volume was at a lower level than he remembered she preferred. There was nothing subdued or understated about her. Just like her apartment. No pastel colors in sight. Bright green and red striped cushions on her navy sofa, loud floral curtains, and orange dishes on the table.

He handed her the bouquet he'd purchased on the way. The array of colorful blooms coordinated with her décor. Other than the sunflowers, he had no idea what they were.

"Thank you. They're lovely." She filled a glass

with water, arranged the flowers, and set them on the table.

"You're not wearing a patch today."

"They're kind of annoying, and I really don't need to wear one. Only a plastic shield at night. Which is also annoying."

"I imagine. When will you be able to get the fancy contact lenses?"

"Not for a couple of months. My doc will advise me."

When Avery arrived a few minutes later, they sat at the round dining table and enjoyed a spicey version of King Ranch chicken casserole, complemented by Avery's tossed salad. Lucas impressed himself by not hesitating once. He even interrupted Avery to add his twenty-two cents worth to an incident they experienced the last time they were in England.

After they cleared away the dishes, Roxanne displayed the items they'd found in Howard's chest. "Isn't this brooch lovely?" She handed it to Avery.

"The York rose. A symbol of Yorkshire which dates back to the Wars of the Roses, between, um, 1455 and 1485. King—"

"Hey, sis. We don't need a history lesson."

"*I* thought it was interesting." Roxy ignored Lucas and set the book of poetry and the locket in front of Avery. "We also found these items. Howard's sister-in-law, Carol Newcombe, had already left so she couldn't identify the photograph."

Avery used her thumbnail to pry out the photo from the locket and turned it over. She squinted. "The name of the photography studio is faint." Grabbing her cell phone, she aimed it at the photo and enlarged the image on the screen. "Aha. Skipton Portraits. I bet we can check it online."

"I'll do that." Roxanne used her phone and within seconds, she'd located the company. "It's on Broughton Road and they're still in business."

"Good. The road runs smack dab through the center of town." Avery bumped Lucas with her elbow. "Why didn't you take the photo out of the locket?"

Why didn't he? He shrugged. Rats. He could have been the hero if he'd paid more attention.

Avery placed the photo back in the locket and Lucas took it from her. "I wonder how old the woman was. Twenty? Older?"

"I've pondered the same question and looked at her many times since we found the locket. If the picture was larger, we'd have a better idea. I think she could have been any age between twenty and thirty-five."

"I agree. What other clues do you have?" Avery asked.

Roxanne handed her the book of poetry. "Read the poem I've marked with a piece of paper. Let us know what you think."

Avery read the short poem, then said, "Wow. Interesting. I have to reread it."

"I had to read it twice before I made a connection

with the title."

A minute passed and Avery closed the book. "She was pregnant."

"My conclusion, too. Carol saw the book one day and noted an inscription inside. 'To my darling Emily Anne' in Benton's handwriting. The page has been torn out."

"Whoa. Hold on a second. Emily Anne?"

"Yes. The name of the woman who accompanied Benton to the ranch."

Avery leaned back, a smug expression on her face. "Well folks, Emily Anne is a lovely name, however…" She looked at Roxanne and then at Lucas.

"What? Don't keep us in suspense." Roxanne wiggled in her seat.

"Another point in Yorkshire's favor. The Brontë sisters lived in Haworth. One was Emily, one Charlotte, and one—"

"Anne. Of course. The woman pictured could have been real clever and used this false name, or her parents were fans of the Brontës." Roxanne's eyes sparkled. "A final clue. Carol mentioned Emily Anne had an unusual English accent."

"The Yorkshire accent certainly fits the bill." Lucas had studied the complexities of the accent along with Avery.

"Oh, one more thing. Carol said Emily Anne always said ta'ra for goodbye and often used the word 'summat' for—"

"Something. Yes. Yorkshire for sure. Certainly a place to start. We can go to Skipton and visit the photographer." Avery massaged her right shoulder. "Ooh, that feels good. Too much driving. Are you ready to book your flight?"

"My surgeon has to clear me first."

"I'm ready to go," Lucas said. "I'll make the arrangements as soon as you let me know, Roxy." He was pleased with himself for offering before Avery did.

Roxanne tilted her head and stared at him. A slow smile touched her face, and if her living room had been any larger, he would have picked her up and twirled her around.

She held out her hand to Lucas. "Locket, please. I wish I hadn't told Tyler about the photo. He…had hard eyes. He didn't seem to look at me but through me. I'm not sure I trust him."

"That's an interesting observation. I found him to be condescending." Lucas's phone rang. A call from Nadine. "I'll take this in the hall." Guessing she'd reiterate her thanks, he said, "Hey, Nadine."

"Thank you again for meeting me yesterday. I'm going back to Houston on Sunday. How about we have lunch tomorrow? Being with you reminded me of what a great guy you are. Considerate, smart. Not to mention as handsome as ever. I'm sorry our relationship ended on a sad note. I'd like to begin again."

Eyebrows raised and mouth agape, he pulled the phone from his ear and stared at it. Her suggestion was definitely unexpected, as he'd never considered their two dates the basis for a relationship. They'd parted as friends, so he had no idea what she meant by a sad note.

"Um, sorry, Nadine. I can't meet tomorrow." He glanced into the dining room, right at Roxanne. "I admire your dedication to your writing, but I think we should keep our relationship on a professional level."

"Rats. I thought you might say that, but I had to try. Blessings on the path you choose."

Still off kilter by Nadine's conversation and not ready to be in Roxanne's company, Lucas remained in the hall. He'd worked so hard with Demetrius, his therapist, and just when he thought he was making progress to be the man Roxanne said she was waiting for, his insecurities came crashing back into his life.

As part of his transformation from wishy-washy to a man of action, Demetrius said Lucas should confront his father about the belittling and humiliating experiences he'd showered on him when a child, but he hadn't been able to yet.

His thoughts raced back to the day Roxanne broke off their relationship. The main reason she gave was his indecisiveness. Seldom making his wants known, always accepting what other people decided. Her final words: "When you learn how to make decisions, how to take the lead sometimes, look me up. I might be waiting for you."

He leaned against the wall and folded his arms. In his defense, he couldn't have reached the age of thirty, working on a PhD without making some decisions along the way, but he understood Roxanne's description of his actions or lack thereof. It had taken him almost a year to realize he needed to change his behavior and mindset. Working with Demetrius had been a blessing.

Squaring his shoulders, he strode into the living room and gave Roxanne a broad smile. He was determined to prove to her he was making changes.

The corners of her mouth turned upward and she nodded.

That was all he needed at the moment.

CHAPTER 6

Before Avery and Lucas left the previous evening, Roxanne had divided the list Howard had given her. Lucas had asked for Wesley Palmer's phone number, reasoning that the nephew might be more forthcoming with a man.

Undaunted that the details might be outdated, she munched on a toasted bagel and smiled. Not only might she contact friends or acquaintances of her father, but she could drive. Six days after surgery, the mere act of being independent again thrilled her. She hollered, "Woohoo!" Good thing she only had a neighbor on one side.

She drained her coffee mug and was about to carry her dishes to the kitchen when her attention was drawn to the flowers Lucas had brought. A speckled, orange tiger lily petal had fallen to the table. She stared at the lilies, blue delphiniums, and red gerbera daisies, then tilted her head. Was Lucas's change in attitude and behavior because she was in a vulnerable state? First the surgery, and then the extraordinary revelation about her mother? Time would tell, especially if the three of them traveled to England. To Yorkshire.

With her dishes placed in the sink, she returned to the table and took photos of the brooch and the picture from the locket with her phone. She emailed them to Petra with a brief description of where they were found. Taking Lucas's advice, she didn't mention the Yorkshire connection.

Avery called, reminding Roxanne to be careful if she located a friend of Benton's. "Meet in a public place, and watch out for other drivers since you only have one eye."

As if she needed a reminder. "Thank you, friend. Don't hang up yet. My parents finally responded to my email when they took a patient to a hospital in Harare. They encouraged me to follow all leads, even if I have to travel to England."

"You have their blessing. That's good news. See ya."

Growing up next door to the Dupree twins was an exciting adventure. Their parents were wealthy. Father excelled in the financial world, and Mother worked in the technology field. Although the kids had every new gadget advertised, they were not snobs and included Roxanne in their world. Her sister and brothers were sometimes invited, but they were several years younger.

Avery and Lucas encouraged Roxanne to join them on many escapades throughout high school. They never flaunted their family's wealth, even when they were given new cars for their seventeenth birthday.

However, when it came time to choose a university, money did play a part. Roxanne's parents, although not in the same financial league as the Duprees, had the means to send their five adopted kids to college. They all attended state universities and worked odd jobs throughout their schooling.

Avery and Lucas chose to attend Rice University in Houston. Now, they were completing the requirements for their PhD programs through the same university, and neither one had a full-time job. Although their parents footed their education bills, the kids didn't squander their time. They had always given back to the community by volunteering at various organizations, a practice they continued. The administration at a local elementary school allowed Avery to use her expertise in phonics to aid the students who struggled to read. Lucas worked at a youth center, assisting teens with weight-lifting and other exercises to improve their wrestling skills. Several boys were hoping to earn college scholarships.

The only negative aspect of the family dynamics Roxanne witnessed as a teenager was Mr. Dupree's attitude toward Lucas. Avery was the favorite, and her father didn't hide the fact. She was beautiful; Lucas had a crooked nose. Avery was outgoing; her brother was shy. When Mr. Dupree didn't know anyone was watching, he'd tear into Lucas, often for no apparent reason. Lucas could never do anything right. Even his choice to join the high school wrestling team met with criticism.

Long after Roxanne broke off her relationship with Lucas, her adult mind scolded her teenage self. His father had brow-beaten Lucas for so long that he quit trying to be independent. He probably found life easier when he followed Avery's suggestions, and later as an adult, he allowed Roxanne to make all the decisions in their relationship because that's all he knew. They'd dated for three years, mostly while she attended the University of Texas campus in San Antonio, and with Lucas in Houston at Rice University, their relationship had little chance to blossom.

The changes she'd witnessed must reflect his breaking away from his life-long residence in Avery's shadow. *Why had Lucas chosen to adjust his behavior close to his thirtieth birthday?*

She hiked a shoulder and sat at the table. Since the twins' schedule was flexible, she appreciated the time they gave her during her recovery and in searching for additional clues to locate her mother. Vision in her left eye was still blurry. She wore a patch whenever she had to read small print. Her list included seven names, one with an address and two with phone numbers. Was eight forty-five on a Saturday morning too early to call? If these people were Benton's contemporaries, they'd be in their 50s or 60s. She dialed the first number. There was no answer, so she left a message stating Howard had given her his name, and she was anxious to learn more about Benton Palmer.

A woman answered the second call.

"Good morning." Roxanne gulped. Leaving a message was easy compared to speaking to someone who might provide information about her father. "My name is Roxanne Clarke. I'm related to Benton Palmer. Is this the correct number for Phillip Long?"

Silence. Then a gasp. "I haven't heard Benton's name for a long time. I'll get Phillip for you. Hold on."

The seconds dragged by, then a gruff, "Who are you?"

"I'm Roxanne, Howard Palmer's granddaughter. He gave me your name and number. Benton was my father."

"I thought he was dead."

"He is, but I was—"

"Listen, little lady. Benton was a sorry excuse of a man."

Roxanne cringed at Phillip's harsh tone. "So I've been told. I was adopted and never met him."

"Good. I'm glad you didn't grow up in his company. Which one of his…who was your mother?"

"That's what I'm trying to discover. Did you know he was married?"

Phillip snorted. "What? I don't believe it."

Although Howard had badmouthed Benton,

Roxanne was offended by Phillip's reaction. "He married in 1997 or '98. Do you, um, know who, which woman he was with then?"

"No."

"Are you sure? Please, I'm desperate."

"I'm sure, missy. He dated my sister in '95. I remember because she turned twenty-five that year. The scoundrel broke her heart, and if he'd hung around town, I'd have broken his neck. So yes, I'm sure. Goodbye."

Roxanne stared at her phone. Call ended. When Phillip's wife had answered, jittery butterflies swarmed in Roxanne's stomach. Now, she swallowed against the bile creeping up her throat. The first contact with someone who knew Benton had been discouraging. If she were able to reach anyone else on the list, she'd better prepare herself for more disappointment.

Social media searches proved futile. If Howard had provided a middle name or initial, Roxanne might have had success. Shoulders hunched, she blew out a sigh. *Do Avery and Lucas have any news?* Her phone rang and she grabbed it. Neither twin's headshot displayed, but the number she'd called earlier. "Hi. Thanks for returning my call. I'm trying to reach Henry Andrews."

"I heard your message. I'm Ivy, his wife. Why do you want information about Benton?"

"He was my father."

Ivy sniggered. "Forgive me, but I can't see Benton as a parent."

"I was adopted and never met him."

"Well, Henry can't help you. He passed away three years ago."

"I'm sorry."

"What do you want to know?"

"I'm trying to find out about my mother. I was born in 1996." Roxanne scrunched up the piece of paper on the table. "Do you know who Benton was seeing at the time?"

"I didn't like him and seldom spent time in his company. No, I don't know."

"Are you aware he married a woman who had his child?"

This time Ivy outright laughed. "Benton married. That's hilarious. You're joking, aren't you?"

"No. I think he married my mother."

"Oh. I'm sorry, my dear. Henry might—hold on a minute. I need to find my old address book." She spoke again a few minutes later. "I've lost touch with Fiona McArthur, but way back, this was her phone number." Ivy rattled off the number which didn't have a San Antonio area code. "She was close to Benton. I hope Fiona can help."

"Thank you so much." Roxanne ended the call and stared at the name she'd written down. She'd seen it recently—on the list she gave Lucas.

He answered her call right away. "Have you had any responses, because I haven't?"

"Yes. I spoke to two people. Neither liked Benton

nor knew anything about his wife. However, the last person I talked to mentioned Fiona McArthur, a name on your list, and provided an old phone number for her."

"Great. You call her and I'll scratch her name off my list. Oh, and I didn't speak to Howard's nephew, but I left a message."

"Even if they weren't close friends, he probably knows more about Benton than Howard assumes." Roxanne ended the call, then with a shaking finger, she tapped Fiona's number.

The phone rang and rang. Finally, a woman with a gravelly voice answered. "Hello."

"My name is Roxanne Clarke. I'm trying to reach Fiona McArthur."

"I'm not in the market for auto coverage or a new cell phone carrier."

Roxanne giggled. "I'm not offering either. I'm Benton Palmer's daughter and hope you can help me."

Silence for a couple of beats. "Benton has a child? I don't believe it."

Her response didn't sound promising. "In fact, he has two. I'm trying to find out the name of my mother. Ivey Andrews gave me your number. She said you and Benton were close."

"We were for a while. What time frame are you interested in?"

"I was born in 1996. Did you know Benton was married?"

Another silence, and then Fiona said, "I did not. No wonder he..." She coughed over and over. "Sorry. Too many years smoking. I remember Benton dropped out of our circle of acquaintances during the mid to late 1990s. We were a wild lot, and, um, sometimes our behavior was antisocial. If that's when he married, maybe he didn't want his bride to associate with his old friends."

"That is a possibility. I have a photograph I believe is of my mother. Can I show it to you? See if you recognize her."

"I suppose. I live in San Marcos. We're celebrating my husband's birthday tonight and our children and grandchildren are coming. I'm free next week."

Roxanne couldn't wait that long. Fiona was the most positive lead she'd found so far. "I hate to impose, but how about tomorrow? I'm really anxious to find my mother."

"I'm not sure..."

"Please. You're my last hope." A bit dramatic, but Roxanne was desperate.

"Oh, I suppose it won't hurt."

"Thank you, thank you. We can meet at a restaurant in San Marcos."

"Okay." She named a place just off Interstate 35. "I'll be available at three o'clock."

"I appreciate you agreeing, Fiona. See you then." Roxanne ended the call and stood, pushing her chair out of the way. She walked to the window and stared at the courtyard surrounded by vegetation. Everything looked so bright and colorful under the Texas sun. The knots in her stomach unraveled and she raised a fist in the air. "Woohoo!"

She called Avery and Lucas to report her discovery and gladly accepted his offer to take them to San Marcos. Although she hated to admit it, she didn't relish driving the fifty miles to the rendezvous.

Lucas hadn't had any success with people or venues on his list. Avery, however, met Jerome Warren, the long-time owner of Cactus Cal's Dance Hall northwest of San Antonio.

"After some prompting, Jerome remembered Benton and his unruly friends. He tolerated their behavior because Benton spent a lot on booze and always made good on any damage his cronies incurred. Jerome said Benton quit attending in the 1990s. He had no information about a wife. In fact, he was surprised to learn Benton had married."

"That agrees with the details I discovered, too." Roxanne rubbed her chin. "Did you meet Jerome or just call?"

"I looked up the dance hall online and called the number listed. Why?"

"Since Benton spent a lot of time there, do you think it would help if Jerome saw the photo in the locket?"

"Let's see what your San Marcos contact says first. Jerome's in the middle of remodeling."

"Okay. See you tomorrow." Roxanne drove to the supermarket to replenish her refrigerator. She also visited an office supply store and had the locket photograph copied and enlarged. Navigating her apartment with one eye was easier than wending through Saturday traffic, but she made it to the shopping center and back in one piece. So much for her independence.

Carrying her purchases and eager to enter her apartment, she paid no attention to a man loitering close to the line of mailboxes for her building. She opened her box, stuffed the junk mail in with her groceries, and headed to her apartment. The man followed her, apparently unconcerned she was aware of his presence. Before she reached the walkway to her apartment, she turned. The man stopped, but this time, she paid close attention. Average height, dark hair partially hidden under a baseball cap worn low over his brow.

"Can I help you?"

He pivoted and disappeared behind the building.

Roxane hurried to her apartment and, once inside, locked the door and leaned against it. Who was he? Why was he following her? A wave of shivers traveled from her shoulders to her toes. "Rats." She should have taken a photo of him.

CHAPTER 7

Antsy and impatient, Roxanne fidgeted all through the church service. She declined a lunch invitation with a group of friends, afraid her preoccupation with meeting Fiona would ruin the day for them.

Humming as she approached her car, she pressed the remote and then froze. Someone had keyed her car. Two almost parallel lines ran from the front fender to the back fender. She touched one of the lines and looked around as if the culprit would be lurking in the parking lot.

Her enthusiasm bubble burst, and she drove home with a dark cloud of anger following her. Who would do such a thing? And only to her vehicle.

To occupy her mind and while away the hours, she answered email, read pertinent articles in medical journals, and finally had a late lunch at her favorite farm-to-table restaurant. How could the time drag by so slowly?

During the drive to San Marcos, she told Lucas and Avery about the damage to her car and the man at her apartment complex.

"Why didn't you call me?" Lucas eyed her in the rearview mirror.

"What good would that have done?"

"Okay, I get your point, but you need to share strange events like that with Avery and me."

She folded her arms and stared at the back of his head. "I will, but I hope there won't be any more 'strange events'."

Lucas parked in the restaurant lot just before three. He'd rented a crew cab pickup. Avery sat in front while Roxanne chose the backseat where there was less glare from the sun. She had the Yorkshire rose brooch, the locket, and the enlarged photo in the satin bag and carried it into the restaurant along with a small notepad.

A woman with hair dyed the color of carrot juice eyed the trio as they entered. She raised a hand and called, "Roxanne?"

"That's me." Roxanne led the way to the table and stuck out her hand. "Fiona, thank you for agreeing to see me. These are my good friends, Avery and Lucas. They're helping in my quest."

"Please join me." Fiona gestured to the waiter. "Would you like something to drink?" She cradled a mug of coffee.

Roxanne and Avery asked for iced tea.

"Just a glass of water." Lucas sat beside Roxanne.

"And a refill of decaf, please." The waiter disappeared behind the partition and Fiona jutted her chin toward Roxanne. "So, young lady, you're Benton's daughter. I can see a slight resemblance, but I still find it hard to believe. He was the least likely one in our group to have kids."

"Were you part of the group who attended Cactus Cal's Dance Hall?" Avery asked.

Fiona's eyebrows rose. "Oh, my. Yes. I hadn't thought of the place for years but Roxanne's call reminded me of many happy nights there, line dancing, two-stepping. Only country music lovers attended back then. Is the place still in business?"

"Yes. I spoke to Jerome Warren who still owns it."

The waiter delivered their drinks, halting the conversation for a few seconds.

"No kidding. He used to get so angry with Benton and his cronies. They were excellent dancers, but after they'd had too many beers, their behavior became disruptive, and Jerome often had to call the police to settle disputes." She let out a deep breath. "Benton was a great guy when he was sober. A good friend."

"Did you know any of his, um, girlfriends?" Roxanne sipped her tea and eyed Fiona over the rim of the glass.

"A few. He didn't seem to stay with anyone very long. Or maybe the women didn't want to stay with *him*. That's probably more like it." Fiona stared off into the distance. "Benton started taking cocaine toward the end of my association with him. Some 'friends' hung around him because he usually paid the tab. And supplied the drugs." She hung her head as if she'd said all she wanted to.

Roxanne removed the locket and enlarged photo from the satin bag. "Howard let us search through a chest full of Benton's belongings. Lucas found a few pieces of jewelry." She opened the locket and handed it to Fiona along with the enlarged copy. "Do you recognize the woman? I'm trying to find out if she was my mother."

Fiona studied the picture and then frowned. "She does look familiar. Too bad her hat covers most of her hair." She stared at Roxanne. "Your hair is an unusual color. There was a woman Benton brought to the hall with beautiful hair, similar to yours. She had a double first name but I don't—"

"Could it have been Emily Anne?" Roxanne held her breath.

"I'm not sure. I was jealous of her, and probably that's why I don't remember. She was short and slender and seemed fragile. Or at least Benton treated her with care as if he loved her." Fiona studied the photo again. "I don't think this is her. When was the photo taken?"

"I don't know. We found this brooch with it." Roxane opened the small box and revealed the white rose.

"The white rose is a symbol of Yorkshire. We have reason to believe the photo was taken there." Avery set her elbows on the table. "Did you by any chance see the woman wearing the brooch?"

Fiona shook her head. "It's been nearly thirty years and I'm sorry, I don't remember. When Benton brought her to the club, I stayed out of his way."

"What makes you think this isn't the woman with Benton?" Lucas asked.

"As I said, she looks familiar but older than I recall." Fiona straightened. "And, unless she gave the locket to Benton—which would be unusual because he wouldn't wear it—why display her own photo in it?"

No one responded for a few seconds. Roxanne looked at Avery, then at Lucas. "Fiona is right. We have no way of knowing. However..." She didn't want to voice the possibility, but she had to. "The picture could be of the woman's mother. My grandmother." If correct, then it might make their quest more difficult.

"That's an interesting idea, Roxy Ruth. If we make it to Yorkshire, we can ask the photographer for the date of the picture."

"Not if, Avery. *When* we...I go to England." Roxanne drained her glass of tea. "Thank you for your time, Fiona." She'd previously written her cell number on a business card and handed it to the woman. "Please get in touch if you think of anything else. Finding the identity of my mother is very important to me."

Lucas paid the tab before they left the restaurant,

and once in the truck, Roxanne huddled in the backseat. Her heart felt like a bowling ball in her chest. Fiona couldn't definitely identify the woman, but the possibility the photo could be of her grandmother opened another drawer in Pandora's box.

Avery leaned over the seat. "How are you, Roxy Ruth?"

"Disappointed about the photo, but Fiona provided insight into my father's character. I now understand why people expressed surprise that he had a child." She waited a moment until she was sure she could continue without her voice cracking. "I'm grateful more than ever that John and Verna adopted me. No telling what my life would be like if Benton had raised me."

Head and heart filled with the "what ifs" of life with Benton or of finding her mother, she jerked when her phone buzzed, indicating a text. She checked the message. "It's from Petra. She says: 'Thank you for the copies of the photo and brooch. I have a lead, but unlike you, I won't share it.' Followed by six exclamation points. I suppose we're better off researching on our own."

"Her comment tells you a bit about her character," Avery said.

"I must admit, when I found out she was my half-sister, I did not do a happy dance." Roxanne drew her legs up onto the seat. "I've been thinking that resembling a person or having a similar color hair won't be enough to prove I'm Benton and Emily Anne's daughter. However, if we locate my mother, we can ask if the baby had any physical abnormality."

"What?" Lucas and Avery asked in unison.

Of course, they wouldn't remember her confession when they were kids. "Many years ago, soon after we met, we were at your pool, barefoot, and you, Lucas, made fun of the odd-shaped toes on my left foot."

"I didn't." He paused, and then added, "Oh, yes, I remember I felt so bad afterward. But in a matter-of-fact manner, you explained your…I've forgotten the name."

"Syndactyly. My big toe and second toe were fused together. The scars are still noticeable, although faint, as is the area on my thigh where a skin graft was taken."

"I'm so sorry I teased you."

Avery swatted his arm. "I must have been inside when that happened. I would have thrown you in the pool if I'd been there. When did you have the surgery, Roxy Ruth?"

"When I was six months old. Only the skin and soft tissue had to be separated. Each toe had its own bone structure."

"You never mentioned the surgery while we dated."

"The topic never arose. Besides, I'd forgotten the incident too until I thought about a legitimate physical identification." Roxanne slipped off her left sandal and massaged her toes. There was a small area of sensitivity along one scar, which she rubbed when sitting barefoot, more out of habit than necessity.

Lucas cleared his throat. "Am I forgiven?"

"Don't be ridiculous. Of course."

"I'm being nosy, but did you go to church this morning?"

Welcoming the change in topic, Roxanne replied, "I certainly did." He'd taken her the previous week, and she'd told him she attended every Sunday she could. She decided to turn the tables. "What about you?" Avery had recently started attending a smaller church close to her condo, and Roxanne wasn't sure if Lucas was still a member of the Faith and Hope Bible Church in their old neighborhood.

"Faith and Hope. Why don't you come and visit next week?"

"Why don't you come with me again?" The invitation slipped out, but once voiced, she was pleased she had.

"Another time, maybe. Do you need to go anywhere else before I take you home?"

"No, thanks. I purchased a few things yesterday. And, my sack was not heavy." She wasn't supposed to lift anything weighing over ten pounds.

Twenty minutes later, he stopped at Roxanne's apartment complex and parked in the visitor area.

"I'll walk with you to your door. If I see any strange men hanging around, I'll chase him down and ask—"

Roxanne chuckled. "If he saw you coming, he'd surrender. Seriously, thank you both for coming with me today. Your support made the results of the trip easier to accept." She climbed out of the truck, headed to her front door, and unlocked it.

"Call if you need anything."

"Thanks again, Lucas."

Before going to bed, she sent Tyler a brief text explaining some of the names Howard provided resulted in a few clues, and reminded him to send Carol's contact info.

That night, she lay in bed and watched the shadows that slipped through the slats of the window blind and danced on her wall. Events that had happened since her surgery flooded her mind like a chaotic storm. She met her grandfather. Knew her father's name.

Should she go to England? Was finding her birth mother or inheriting the estate so important? On the other hand, Petra's mother could have married Benton. However, it seemed Carol Newman and Fiona thought Roxanne's hair was a similar color to the woman seen with Benton. So much depended on the identity of the woman in the photograph.

Hmm. How could she use the money to help others if she was the legitimate heir? She already worked with children with special needs and could establish a camp for the kids. With horses and dogs. Equine therapy. Mind racing with possibilities, her heart almost stopped when a noise from the kitchen interrupted her fantasy.

She eased out of bed and tiptoed to her desk. What could she use as a weapon? Nothing. Enough light from the parking area shone through the kitchen window to illuminate the room. There was someone in her kitchen. She sucked in a breath. What should she do? Her phone was charging in the bathroom out of reach. Where could she hide? In the closet? No. The door hinges squeaked. Under the bed? Not enough—

Another noise from the living room this time and the next thing she knew, a flashlight shone right in her eyes.

"Hey, what do you want?" She blinked and turned her head.

The intruder entered her bedroom, pushed her onto the bed, and said, "Stay there. Don't scream, and I won't hurt you."

His voice seemed unnaturally gruff as if he deliberately lowered it. He moved the flashlight around and Roxanne noted he wore dark clothes, a ski mask, a baseball cap, and gloves.

"What did you take from Benton's chest?"

That's the last demand she expected to hear. Insides quivering like a puppy in a thunderstorm, she hesitated to reply. She knew exactly where the book of poetry and scarf were, but where had she put the jewelry bag when she came home? With the other items?

The man stepped closer and loomed over her. "Did you hear me?"

She nodded. Too scared to lie, she stammered, "A book and…and a scarf. And—"

"Is that all? Where are they?"

"On my desk." She rose slowly.

He waved the light across the piece of furniture and grabbed the items. Once he had them in hand, he pushed her. She stumbled and fell onto the bed.

In a flash, he was out the front door.

Roxanne gasped in air. When she came home from San Marcos, she'd set the satin bag beside the scarf, something she'd forgotten in her state of fear. She crawled to the wall, turned on the light, and glanced at her desk. No book, no scarf. She gulped. No jewelry bag, either.

CHAPTER 8

Receiving a phone call from Roxanne at four in the morning, Lucas's danger meter. He rubbed his eyes and asked, "What happened, Roxy?"

"A man broke into my apartment and…and took the items we found in the chest. I gave up too easily. He knew all about our search. And now I don't have the photo." She panted as if out of breath. "I might as well quit."

"First, Roxy, did he hurt you?"

"No. The police have already been here. Did the fingerprint thing, especially around the kitchen window."

"Is that where he got in?"

"Yeah. But I told them he wore gloves."

Her voice conveyed more anxiety than her words did. "I'll be there in fifteen minutes. In the meantime, take deep breaths and relax."

What a senseless thing to say. Relax. Yeah, right.

He dressed and drove to her apartment.

Roxy opened the door at his knock. "I checked the peephole first. Come, sit." She settled on the sofa, her legs drawn up. "Thanks for coming. Is this what you call a strange event?"

"Yes, but more dangerous than strange." He sat beside her. "Were you able to describe him?"

"Average height. But his face was covered and he wore a baseball cap."

"Roxy, do you have any teabags?"

Frowning, she pointed to the last cabinet in the kitchen. "Only herbal."

"Good. I'll make you a cup of hot, sweet tea. Mother always said that was a remedy for shock." He set two mugs of water in the microwave and found the box of tea. "What favor?"

"Peach, please."

"Coming right up." The microwave dinged, he removed the mugs and placed a tea bag in each. Then added two spoonsful to her mug. "Here. And I brought a bowl for the used bags."

"Thanks. You think of everything."

Even considering the circumstances, he basked in her praise. "I'm glad you called me. Now, let's figure out how to remedy this situation. You have no photo, but you sent a copy to Petra. Did you take a picture of it with your phone?"

"Of course. It's still there. I can print another copy"

"One problem solved. Finish your tea, then show me where you had the items."

A few minutes later, they entered her bedroom, and she pointed to her desk. "I tossed everything there when I came home yesterday."

The surface of her desk was as tidy as if being used in a photo shoot. He expected no less. "It's not flush with the wall."

"My lamp and laptop charger are plugged into the outlet behind it."

"I imagine things have fallen off the edge."

"Let's find out. Pull it away from the wall."

He picked up one end and moved it forward, and then did the same with the other end. Furniture on carpet didn't slide.

Roxy was right at his side and she looked behind the desk. "Oh, thank the Lord. There's the satin bag. A notepad, a couple of pens." She retrieved the bag and sank onto the bed. "Lucas, you are a genius. I could kiss you."

She turned a lovely shade of rose. He almost said, "Why don't you?" But he knew it was just an off-the-cuff saying. "Glad to be of service." He bowed and then laughed. "I think we need to find a secure hiding place."

"Um, a safety deposit box at my bank?"

"Perfect. Get dressed, then we can stop for breakfast, and be at your bank when it opens."

Several hours later, Roxanne had placed the

jewelry in her newly acquired safety deposit box. On the way home, she received a phone call.

She checked the caller ID. "It's my clinic. I hope my substitute isn't quitting. Hello."

She mumbled uh-huh a few times, glanced at Lucas, face ashen, and ended the call."

"What's happened?"

She cleared her throat. "Um, a parent is threatening to sue me for giving the wrong medication to his child." Her voice broke, and she placed a hand on his arm. "Please take me to the clinic."

"Sure." He turned up a side street, circled the block, and headed to the clinic.

After he parked, she didn't get out of the truck.

"Do you want me to go in with you?"

She nodded and waited for him to open her door. On any other occasion, she would have been out of the truck before he unbuckled his seatbelt.

He noted she walked with a straight back and her chin up. By her body language, no one would suspect her earlier defeatist demeanor.

The receptionist directed them to an office at the end of a long hall. "Ms. Ingram will be with you shortly."

"And she is…?"

"Supervisor of the whole clinic."

They sat down in the small outer office, but soon her door opened. "Come in Miss Clarke, but you sir, will have to wait out here. We'll be discussing confidential formation."

"Fine." He understood the reasoning, but that didn't stop him from sending moral support in a prayer. The meeting took all of fifteen minutes.

Roxy walked out with a grim expression on her face. He followed her to the truck, where she stood as if in a trance. "Hey, kid, want to talk?"

"No. Please take me home."

Silence reigned in the cab, but Lucas knew better than to prod Roxy. She'd tell him about the meeting when she was ready. He walked with her to her apartment and entered behind her. "You've had a rough morning. Can I do anything for you before I leave?"

She dumped her purse on the dining table and set her hands on her hips. "Could you tell I was fuming in the truck? I have to vent. Can you stay, please?"

"How about I make us more tea?"

"Thanks."

When the mugs were ready, he carried them to the sofa where she'd settled.

She sipped her tea and stared off into the kitchen. "I trust you not to divulge anything I tell you. Not even to Avery. The parent in question wants to sue me for malpractice. I can't believe it. His son has been a patient with us for three or four years. I've seen him many times. He's a lovely kid."

"Why is the parent doing this? Because I know you and the last thing you'd do is give a patient the wrong meds."

She hiked a shoulder and bit her bottom lip.

"Do you have their address? Could you talk to the parent?"

"That's not a good idea." She set her empty mug on the coffee table. "I think I'll wait until I've spoken to a lawyer. The clinic has legal representatives to handle their issues. Remember, we're just one location in the corporation."

"But their lawyers will have the corporation's interests in sight."

"I guess I'll have to hire one. That'll be expensive."

"Don't worry about money. Do what will help you prove your innocence. Avery and I will be honored to help."

"I'll wait until I've met with the board. Wednesday at ten."

"I have an appointment at Rice in Houston. I'll be gone a couple of days, but I can reschedule."

She drew her legs up onto the sofa, such a characteristic move, he should have expected it.

"No. Don't do anything to mess with your program. I'll be fine by myself."

No doubt she would be, but he so wanted her to need him.

Her phone pinged. "Hey, it's a text from Tyler. I hope he has—no, no."

"What?"

"Carol passed away last night. She fell, hit her

head, and never regained consciousness." Roxy thumped a cushion. "That is so sad."

"Do you want me to stay?"

"No, thanks."

He stood and made his way to the door, then turned. "Hey, have you told the superintendent about the break-in?"

"Not yet, but he should have known something was wrong when the cops showed up."

"I'll tell him now, and insist he replace all the window locks for the ground floor apartments."

"Thanks."

Dark circles underlined her eyes. "You need to rest. How much sleep did you get last night?"

She yawned as if to emphasize his point. "None."

"So…off to bed, you go. I won't leave until you're under the covers."

"Yes, sir, Mr. Dupree." She gave him a salute, entered her bedroom, and closed the door. "You can go now."

He chuckled. Roxy had a way of getting in the last word.

The superintendent agreed to replace the locks, starting with Roxanne's apartment. On the way home, he stopped at the law firm where his parents had an account. The bigwigs weren't available, so he was ushered into a junior partner's office and relayed all he knew about Roxanne's situation.

Elaine Ryland tapped a pen on her desk. "The best

advice I can give on such meager information is to tell Miss Clarke to Document all pertinent actions or conversations, including the meeting today. Tape record her meeting with the board, with their knowledge. After they've laid down their cards, she'll know how the parent wants to proceed, which will determine her next move."

"Thank you, Ms. Ryland. I appreciate you seeing me on such short notice."

"Your parents are valued clients. A few more questions. Has Miss Clarke been given a leave of absence? Do you trust her?"

"I have complete faith in her. She would never harm anyone, let alone a patient. And no, she's on medical leave at the moment due to surgery."

Ms. Ryland pulled a folder from a desk drawer. "I'll open a case file for her. Let me know what occurs with the board."

Lucas stood and offered his hand to her. "Thank you. I will."

Walking to his truck, he contemplated texting Roxy about his visit to the lawyer but decided against it. As independent as she was, she might not appreciate his action. He prayed Ms. Ryland's expertise wouldn't be needed. But as soon as he sat behind the wheel, he recalled her advice to Roxy.

Fine. He texted her and included the advice—document all and tape record the board meeting. Her next call to him would probably burn off his ears.

CHAPTER 9

The nap accomplished its purpose. Roxanne awoke with a clearer picture of how she could combat the possible lawsuit. First, she'd visit Mr. Naylor and ask for details. He might not welcome her visit, and he certainly wouldn't have appreciated Lucas's. Then, she'd review her notes in Gary's file.

About to walk out the door, she checked her phone. Two missed calls and a text from Lucas. What now? She hoped he didn't cancel his meeting in Houston. She read his words and sat at the dining table. Why did he visit a lawyer? To help her, of course. But couldn't he have waited for her to ask? She thumped the table. What a pickle. She had to admit the lawyer's advice was valuable. Could she trust the higher-ups at the clinic? She had in the past, but she'd never been accused by a parent of malpractice before.

She replied to Lucas with a curt, *Thank you.* and

proceeded to her car. Ugh, the scratches would have to wait. She scanned the area and noticed no strange men ready to commit strange events.

Fred Naylor lived in the next subdivision. Gary had been her patient long enough for her to know his address. She parked in the driveway and slowly approached the front door. It opened before she knocked.

"What do you want?" Mr. Naylor held the door open enough to stick out his head.

"Please tell me why you're doing this. I would never knowingly give a patient the wrong meds or meds that aren't prescribed. How is Gary?"

"Big questions for a little lady. You shouldn't be here. I have a restraining order against you. I could call the cops but I won't this time. Bye." He slammed the door in her face.

Restraining order. Getting serious. She swallowed hard and drove home. Mr. Naylor's expression and tone of voice left no doubt he was adamant about the accusation.

Seated at her desk, she reread Lucas's text and jotted down the name of the lawyer he consulted and the address of the building. She might need her services.

Roxanne opened her laptop to log into the portal used by the clinic. She tried her password three times with no success. They'd locked her out. She had no other way to check her notes on Gary's last visit.

Closing her eyes, she recalled the visit a few days before her eye surgery. As usual, Fred brought him into her room. He was physically thirteen, with many characteristic features of a person with Down syndrome. He was charming, funny, and had a mischievous smile.

Gary had been on medication for epilepsy for years, and every six months, Roxanne performed a routine exam to make sure the dosage was correct for his age and weight. However, at that visit, he had a respiratory infection. She prescribed amoxicillin, an antibiotic that Gary had taken previously with quick results and no side effects.

That was it.

She paced in her small bedroom, muttering, "What else? Nothing. Routine visit." She stopped and pictured her consulting room. The usual medical equipment and models of internal body parts, such as the ear, the chest, and the heart. Most of her young patients loved examining them. Gary was no exception. His favorite was the model of the heart.

There was no medication in her room. Not even over-the-counter products. When she had the antibiotics in hand, she called Fred into the room and personally gave him the pack of chewable tablets the pharmacist had delivered. Gary couldn't swallow anything bigger than a pea.

"Argh," she yelled. "What went wrong?" Could Gary have picked up something off the floor in the hall or waiting room? Highly unlikely. The staff knew to keep all meds in a locked cabinet and to never leave the patient alone in a consulting room.

By now, Roxanne had a headache that pommeled her brain like a battering ram. Dehydrated, no nourishment since her early breakfast, and enough drama to qualify for a daytime soap opera script.

The next morning, she called Elaine Ryland and scheduled an appointment for Friday morning. By then, she'd have a recording of the board meeting and, hopefully, actions or events they could dispute.

Roxanne determined she wouldn't dwell on the upcoming meeting all day. Instead, she called Avery who came over a few hours later.

"What's new, Roxy Ruth?"

She hugged her friend and then plopped onto the sofa. "Nothing. Did Lucas tell you about my problem at the clinic?"

"He did. I know you wouldn't do anything to harm a patient. What is the father trying to accomplish?"

"I don't know. He even has a restraining order against me. And…I've been locked out of the clinic's portal. I can't check any records, or…" She huffed out a breath. "And, now we can't go to Yorkshire until this legal mess is concluded."

"That could take a long time."

"I know. Just when I thought we had a positive lead."

"Ah, come here, chickadee." Avery drew her into a hug. "We'll get there."

"Eventually. It may not be until December. Does it snow in Yorkshire?"

Avery released her and burst out laughing. "Does it ever. We don't want to travel there in winter. However, I have a great idea. How about we go shopping? I haven't bought a new outfit in months."

Who could resist a shopping spree with Avery? She had great fashion taste, and Roxanne always came home with something she'd never have chosen for herself.

Time spent with her best friend and acquiring a few blouses, put Roxanne in a pleasant mood. When she awoke the next morning, she was still on a cloud. Maybe not nine, but close enough.

She dressed with care in a royal blue short-sleeve pantsuit and twisted her hair at her nape to form an old-fashioned bun. During the drive, she repeated her prayer for wisdom on how to resolve the situation. Walking calmly into the clinic took all of her willpower. She kept repeating the words from Lucas's text that morning. "You are not the person he says you are."

At last, the receptionist beckoned her. "They're ready for you. Do you know where to go?"

Most definitely. She took the stairs up to the third

floor and entered the conference room. She was shown to a chair at one end. The other people in the room were not strangers, but no one smiled or made eye contact. Hmm.

As she sat, she pulled out her phone. "I'll be recording the meeting."

Beverly Ingram said, "I will also record the meeting." She set out her phone and cleared her throat. "We will begin. As you are aware, Miss Clarke, serious charges have been brought against you. Mr. Fred Naylor has stated that at Gary's last visit to the clinic two weeks ago, you gave him medication that later made him ill enough to visit the ER."

Roxanne frowned. "Wait, wait. I never gave Gary anything. I handed the prescribed antibiotics to Mr. Naylor personally."

"Did you prescribe them?"

"Yes. And signed off by Dr. Ortiz, which is all documented in Gary's file."

"We have checked and find you are correct, however—"

"This is a major point, " added Dr. Joanne Hill, an on-call ENT.

Roxanne raised her brows. Must be important for her to pipe in.

"Mr. Naylor stated you took pills out of your scrubs pocket and gave them to Gary."

Taken aback, Roxanne looked at each member of the board, then focused on Beverly. "I did no such thing, nor would I ever give a patient random pills from my...pocket. I don't even carry candy."

"Any proof?"

"Other than my impeccable record and my word, no."

"Any witnesses?"

Her anger built and she forced her tone to be civil. "The CNA was with me the whole time."

"Who was it?"

"Um. I can't recall...oh, yes. The new guy. My mind's a blank. I don't remember his name, but it's in my notes."

"Continue."

"When I left the room to submit the script to the pharmacy, the CNA remained with Gary. When I returned, he had to go to another patient, but that's when I invited Mr. Naylor in."

"Another point we want on the records is that this incident took place a few days before your surgery. Were you distracted? Mind not on the job?"

"That is an insult to my professionalism. I take my job seriously, as my colleagues can confirm. I'd researched the surgery and knew what to expect. I am always focused on the patient. Always."

"Anything else?"

Roxanne took in a few deep breaths. Anything else? Was Beverly joking? She had a dozen points she wanted Mr. Naylor to clarify. Too bad he was not present. She did have a couple of questions that needed answers now.

"What happened to Gary in the ER? Is he all right? What meds was he given?"

"All in good time. We'll consider your testimony and get back to you in a few days."

Roxanne rolled her eyes. A few days? Why not? She had all the time in the world.

"Am I free to go?"

"One more item, you're on administrative leave until further notice."

"Fine. At our next meeting, I will bring my lawyer." She had to squelch the desire to storm out, and she took measured steps to the door and, this time, used the elevator. She didn't think she could manage the stairs without collapsing.

Lucas and Avery had both asked for an update after the meeting, but that was the last thing Roxanne felt like doing. She drove home, kicked off her shoes, and removed her jacket. No sooner had she sat down and her phone rang. She didn't recognize the number but answered anyway. "Hello."

Silence, not even background noise.

"Hello. Who's this?"

"The items I took from your apartment were not helpful. Where's the photo? Don't bother tracing this phone. I'll toss it when you hang up."

She almost threw her phone across the room. *Now that's what I call a strange event.* "I might as well call Lucas." He could still be in Houston, but she'd leave him a message. Which she did. Knowing his protective nature, he'd return her call as soon as possible.

Thinking of Lucas reminded her to update Elaine Ryland. She forwarded the recording of the meeting to the lawyer and was surprised when she called a half-hour later.

"Thank you for the recording, When we meet on Friday, we'll fill in any gaps surrounding this alleged incident. In the meantime, if you have any questions, please call or text."

Lucas was right. Elaine's confident and calming voice alleviated some of Roxanne's anxiety. Having someone on her side reassured her she would get through this dark cloud.

With time on her hands, Roxanne dropped off her car at the dealership, signed for a rental, and visited the rock climbing club. She'd only been a member for a few months, attending when her schedule and church obligations allowed. This was the first time since her surgery that she felt ready to visit, although her surgeon had okayed the exercise a few days ago. She checked that all her gear was in her gym bag and hurried to her car. The physical activity would take her mind off her problems.

She was still considered a novice and spent a couple of hours perfecting a few skills. Her busy life, up until now, prevented her from climbing often enough to progress faster. But the workout suited her fine. After all, she wasn't about to climb the Rockies.

Lucas called as soon as she arrived home. She remained in the car and described the phone call from the intruder.

"No way to trace it?"

"That's what he said."

"Do you want to move in with Avery? She won't mind."

"No, thanks. He'll still be able to call me there."

"Yeah, but you won't be alone at night. Do you always answer calls without a caller ID?"

"Not usually, but I won't in future. If they are legit callers, they can leave a message."

"Exactly. I'll be home later this evening. Call if—"

"Thanks. I will." No sooner had she ended the call than her phone rang. No caller ID, so she let it go to message. A few minutes later she listened to it.

"Just because you don't answer, doesn't mean I'll forget. Where's the photo?"

This little charade went on for hours, with a total of four calls. Always a different number, but the message mirrored the first one. She finally turned off her phone and went to bed.

Besides the annoying phone calls, nothing exciting happened in her world until she received a letter from the clinic stating the next meeting was scheduled for the following Monday.

She immediately texted Elaine and then sent the same message to Avery and Lucas.

CHAPTER 10

The meeting with the lawyer put Roxanne's mind at ease. Elaine might be a junior member of the law firm, but she exuded confidence which spilled over and calmed Roxanne's soul. She'd prayed often for wisdom to know what to do, and following Elaine's advice was an answer.

The weekend dragged by as if the hours had accumulated roll-over minutes. Another visit to the rock-climbing club and the church service helped get her through with her sanity intact.

Lucas insisted he drive her to the clinic and arrived Monday morning with a bouquet of bright pink carnations.

"Thank you. They're lovely."

"I purchased them yesterday and used a tiny pair of scissors to snip the edges of the little petals."

Roxanne frowned and looked at him. She read the

mischief in his eyes and playfully slapped his shoulder. "You joker. But thanks for adding levity to my day." She placed the flowers in a vase and set it on the table.

When they arrived at the clinic, Elaine met them at the reception counter.

"Thank you for coming." Roxanne shook her hand but felt like hugging the woman, too.

"They're ready for you, Miss Clarke." The receptionist barely made eye contact with Roxanne.

They rode the elevator up to the third floor.

"Lucas, you'll have to—"

"I know."

The elevator doors opened and Lucas turned left to a small waiting area, and Roxanne and Elaine entered the conference room.

Seated around the oblong table, were the same people as last time. There were two vacant chairs opposite Roxanne.

She addressed the supervisor, Beverly Ingram, and introduced Elaine.

As done at the previous meeting, Beverly set her phone on the table. "I'll record this meeting when all participants are present."

"Who are the other attendees?" Elaine set a small recorder on the table.

"I'll introduce them when they arrive."

Roxanne had a good idea they were waiting for Fred and Gary Naylor. She texted their address to Lucas and asked him to check their home.

Every participant glanced at the large clock on the west wall at least once including Roxanne. No one spoke for a while until Elaine cleared her throat.

"I have another engagement later this morning. Can we begin without the absentees? I have information to share that will affect the outcome of this meeting."

Beverly addressed the board members. "Any objections to Ms. Ryland's request?"

An echo of "no" circled the room.

"You may proceed."

"Thank you. My investigator visited the ER where Gary Naylor was treated. Naturally, he had no access to the boy's file. However, he was able to collect details that will exonerate my client."

Roxanne had no idea about these details, but the word 'exonerate' lifted her spirits.

"Continue, Ms. Ryland," Beverly said.

She opened a file and removed several pages. "While asking questions about Gary in the ER, a woman approached my investigator and indicated she was in the facility with her son at the same time as Mr. Naylor. Her son has a chronic illness and often needs emergency care. At that visit, they were in neighboring rooms. She recognized Gary because he attends some classes with her son, and he's the only student in that grade with Down syndrome."

"This is all hearsay. We—"

"But if my client goes on trial, we will include this woman on our witness list. I'll continue. She overhead conversions from Gary's room. She admitted to eavesdropping and peeking around the curtain, but in her defense, she added their voices were loud. Each time a nurse asked the patient questions, Mr. Naylor responded. Finally, the nurse requested that Mr. Naylor allow Gary to answer. Which he did in between giggles."

Elaine turned to the next page. "I apologize, but this is a lengthy report. When the nurse asked where the pain was, Gary said, 'My tummy.' He moaned and moaned and writhed on the bed. The nurse asked, 'Does your tummy hurt?' Gary moaned again but said, 'No. Here on my side. But don't touch 'cause it tickles.' Mr. Naylor was heard muttering in the background. When the doctor examined Gary, his pain had moved to his lower chest."

Leaning toward Roxanne, Elaine said, "Please hand me a bottle of water."

Roxanne reached for two bottles, gave one to the lawyer, and took a gulp from the other bottle.

"Thanks." She sipped the water. "The woman added that whenever staff members entered the room, Gary moaned and wriggled on the bed, but when they left, he was still and quiet. The doctor shook his head as he walked out of the room. Maybe he agreed with her that Gary's visit to the ER was bogus. He wasn't kept in very long, and when he strolled down the hall, he smiled and joked with the staff."

The lawyer looked at the big clock. "How long do

we wait? I need to leave soon, and recommend we postpone the meeting."

"My secretary has been calling our guests, but there's no answer."

As if on cue, the door opened, and in walked Fred and Gary. Lucas stood in the doorway and smiled at Roxanne. She mouthed, "Thank you."

Beverly introduced the Naylors and indicated where they should sit. "We have additional questions, Mr. Naylor."

Shifting in his chair as if it were covered in ants, he shrugged. "I did it for my son."

"Excuse me. Did what?" Roxanne had never heard Beverly raise her voice before.

He rubbed his neck and hung his head. "A man gave me…money to accuse Miss Clarke." He glanced at her. "Sorry, I was desperate."

"What man?" Dr. Ortiz asked.

"He told me his name was John Smith. I know, probably not his real name."

"How did he pay you?"

"Cash."

"Did he tell you why?"

Dr. Ortiz had taken over the meeting.

"He did not. He told me what to say and do. I'm ashamed I followed his instructions."

"Did Gary have a medical need to go to the ER?"

Fred shook his head. "Ask Gary."

The boy smiled at everyone. "What's your

question?"

"When you went to the emergency room, did you have stomach pains?" Dr. Ortiz rubbed his abdomen. "Here."

"What's a emergency room?"

"Let's try another question. You know Miss Clarke, right?" He pointed to Roxanne and she waved to Gary.

"Yes, but she's my doctor. Call her Dr. Clarke."

"I will. Did *Dr. Clarke* give you pills she took out of her pocket?"

If his glare was anything to go by, elevating Roxanne to Dr. Clarke must have injured his brain.

"No, not even candy. She doesn't have anything to eat in her room. Nothing. Dad, can we go now? I'm hungry."

Roxanne drew in a deep breath and hid a smile. A couple of members chuckled. Gary was always hungry.

Elaine stacked papers and slipped them into the folder. "Does Mr. Naylor's testimony absolve my client.?"

"For the record, Mr. Naylor, did you fabricate the details about Miss Clarke giving Gary unprescribed medication that caused you to take your son to the ER?" Dr. Ortiz glared at the man over the rim of his glasses.

"I did. And again, Miss Clarke—"

"Dr. Clarke, Dad. You must be respect."

"Yes, son. I will be respectful. Dr. Clarke, I apologize for trying to ruin your reputation. You have always been an excellent provider, and Gary loves you."

Gary hunched his shoulders. "I love my Dr. Clarke."

She smiled at him and nodded. Although his words cleared her name, they also sent a ripple of unease through her body. *Ruin my reputation?* Wouldn't that be something the person desperately trying to get his hands on the jewelry bag might do? Why? To delay her quest. To keep her in Texas.

"Miss Clarke." Beverly repeated, "Miss Clarke."

Roxanne blinked. She was already on her way to England. "Yes."

"We will clear your file of any reference to this unfounded lawsuit. You may return to work when cleared by your doctor."

They probably expected her to smile and thank them and be grateful. But she scooted back her chair and stood. "I'm thankful my reputation is intact, but I won't return for a while. I will use up all my vacation days and travel."

To England. To Yorkshire.

CHAPTER 11

Three Weeks Later:

The drone of the airplane engines filled the cabin. Lucas had an aisle seat, Roxanne sat in the middle, and Avery dozed in the window seat huddled under her blanket. The overnight flight to England would take eight hours, landing in Manchester at seven the next morning.

Lucas leaned toward Roxanne. "Are you comfortable?"

"Yes, but I'm too excited to sleep."

"Same here. Avery can nap anywhere." He shifted in the seat and stretched out his legs. Economy Plus was worth every penny.

Roxanne looked in her purse again, clutched it to her body, and sighed.

"The jewelry bag is still there?"

"Of course. I haven't let it out of my sight since I took it from my security box at the bank."

"I know. I've watched you." He placed his hand over hers on the armrest, and she didn't pull away. "You've endured so many upheavals since finding the locket. But, here we are, on our way to Yorkshire."

She set her purse at her feet and nudged it toward her backpack. "I still think about the night the man broke into my apartment. I'm thankful the bag slid off my desk."

"Although the superintendent has replaced the locks on your windows, have you thought any more about moving?"

"I'll leave that decision until we return to Texas." She wrapped her arms around herself and shivered. "I'm getting cold."

He removed the plastic cover from her blanket and draped it across her. "Too bad the intruder left no prints. But you weren't hurt. That's most important."

"I suppose."

He turned off their overhead lights. "Are you satisfied with the contract nurse filling in for you at the clinic?"

"Yeah. He's had years of experience and fits in well with the staff. The nurse who worked while I was on medical leave couldn't stay. I think the bigwigs are happy I'm not there right now. If I met them in the hall, I'm sure no one would make eye contact." She drew up her knees and tucked the blanket around her legs.

"That's their loss. By the way, has Tyler ever responded to your texts?"

"He's a man of few words, and I've followed his lead. I told him I was going to England but never mentioned Yorkshire. I figure the updates are more for Howard's benefit than Tyler's."

"He doesn't need to know every move we make."

She nodded. "I'm so disappointed that Wesley Palmer never returned your call."

"I left several messages indicating why I wanted to connect."

"Lucas," she looked at him, "is this trip a wild goose chase? Am I delusional in thinking I can find my mother?"

The cabin lights dimmed and Lucas leaned closer. Her long hair cascaded over her shoulders, her wide, dark eyes searched his face and she bit her bottom lip. She didn't know how beautiful she was. "Roxy, this trip is not in vain. The evidence points to Yorkshire, and I believe we must follow the clues. We might not find your mother, but you'd never forgive yourself if you didn't try."

She nodded. "You're right. Thanks for the encouragement."

Ever since Roxanne met her grandfather, she'd warmed to Lucas little by little. He was finding it easier to be in her company without a predetermined list of decisions he might make. He'd met with Demetrius twice since Roxy's surgery, and the therapist complimented him on his progress and successful encounters with her.

The time in England would necessitate they'd be in close proximity—staying in the same hotel, riding in a car together, eating meals, and plotting. After a couple of weeks focused on one outcome, Lucas was sure she would mellow even more. Maybe to the level that would convince her to renew their relationship. He huffed out a breath and reclined his seat. A man could dream, couldn't he?

A gentle pressure on his upper arm brought him back to reality. He turned toward Roxanne. She'd fallen asleep, and her head rested on his shoulder. Ahh. He lay back, closed his eyes, and smiled. After she'd ended their relationship, Lucas figured rekindling it was nigh on impossible. Her head on his shoulder was a minor gesture, but his heart rate accelerated anyway.

The train from Manchester Airport to Skipton in Yorkshire arrived on time. Avery had convinced Roxanne that a carry-on suitcase and her backpack were all she needed. Before she objected, Lucas hooked her case onto his and followed the signs to the exit and the parking area where he signed for their rental car. He'd reserved a sedan at the same time he'd booked their flights. A smart move as they were traveling at the height of the tourist season.

Roxanne set her backpack in the trunk beside their suitcases and said, "Train travel seems popular in England."

"Yup. The British sure know how to do mass transportation." Avery climbed into the backseat.

Lucas clipped his seatbelt and started the engine. When he and Avery were in England doing research for their degree requirements, they seldom visited the same locations. They each rented cars and became very familiar with the satnav system, which used postcodes to guide them to their destinations. He looked at her in the rearview mirror. "Avery, do you have the postcode for the photography studio handy?"

"Yeah, it's on my phone, but I'm famished. Let's have lunch first."

"Good idea. My stomach's rumbling as if it's running on empty." Roxanne zipped up her jacket. "I'm not complaining, but it's certainly cooler than Texas."

Lucas eased into traffic, mindful to keep on the left side of the road. "Daytime temps will probably be in the high 60s. Cooler if it's overcast." He slowed. "How about Thai food?" Without waiting for a response, he pulled into the restaurant's parking area.

As they entered the café, Avery whispered to him, "I'm proud of you."

Smiling, he slipped into the booth the waiter indicated. Yeah. Since boarding the plane, he'd been faced with countless decisions, big and small, and so far, he hadn't hesitated once. He wondered if Roxanne had noticed.

They didn't talk much during the meal and were soon on their way to Skipton Portraits.

David Saunderson, the owner, studied the small photograph Roxanne handed him. He turned it over. "It's certainly one of ours."

"Do...do you have the woman's name?" she asked.

"When was the picture taken?"

"At least twenty-eight years ago. Would you like to see an enlarged copy?"

David raised an eyebrow. "No, thank you. I'll use the ID number on the back. When my father ran the business, he insisted employees keep immaculate records. Paper records. I'll check his filing system." The portly man dressed in a dark suit exited through a door at the rear of the shop.

Roxanne studied the large portraits on the walls, Avery sat on a bench beside the counter, rubbing lotion on her arms and hands, and Lucas jingled the car keys. He wanted to put his arm around Roxy's tense shoulders but held back. Not the right time or place.

Returning fifteen minutes later, David frowned as he approached the counter. "Not exactly good news, I'm afraid."

"Why? What did you discover?" Roxanne hurried to the counter.

"The identification number on the photo is not complete. The last two digits are missing as if they were cut off."

Roxanne removed the locket from her purse. "So the picture could fit in here."

"Aha. I have the names of four women who are possibilities. The photos were taken in 1994 and 1995." He handed a piece of paper and one of his business cards to Roxanne. "I included their contact details, but remember, the information is thirty years old. However, people in our smaller towns and villages tend to live in the same homes for a long time."

"Thank you so much. I think this woman is my mother." Roxanne backed away and clutched the paper to her chest.

"We appreciate your help, Mr. Saunderson." Lucas slipped his arm around her shoulders this time and ushered her out the door.

She sniffed and smiled up at him. "None of the women is Emily Anne."

"I'm sure that's disappointing. But one might be your grandmother."

Avery walked beside Roxanne. "Let me see the names." She scanned the paper. "Their addresses include postcodes. Good. Of course, the ladies might not live there any longer. And the phone numbers provided were probably landlines, and who knows if they are still active. Only one way to find out. Let's visit Alicia Maynard. She has a local address. The next two are or were in villages northwest of Skipton; one is Settle, and the other is Grassington. Hey, Roxy, Lucas and I accumulated a lot of information on dialects when we worked in that area last year." She stopped at the car and tapped the page. "The fourth woman has an address in Pateley Bridge. I don't know where that is. Hey, Roxy Ruth, we could call and ask if Alicia traveled to Texas or if her daughter did."

"We could, but I'd rather meet the woman, and see if I recognize any features."

Settled behind the wheel, Lucas entered the postcode into the satnav system. "Only a mile and a half away." He glanced at Roxanne. Her hands were tightly clasped in her lap. "Are you all right?"

"Everything that has happened since my surgery six weeks ago has cemented together to weigh me down from my head to my feet. I can't think clearly, I don't know if I'm happy or sad. My heart feels as if it's filled with lead. I'm grateful for you guys accompanying me because I don't think I could do this on my own."

That admission took a lot coming from Roxanne, the most "in control" person he'd ever met. "Avery and I are fortunate to be in a position to help you. Besides, we'll conduct more research while in Yorkshire."

"Yeah. I've been in touch with Opal Carr, the president of a local historical society. She lives in Kendal, not far from Settle. She recently informed me she found two journals detailing the progression of the use of certain phrases and pronunciation of letters in a family unit going back a century. I had no idea we'd be in that area, so I'll contact her to see if we can meet. She was going to mail them, but now she won't have to."

"And I'll contact a professor at York University who has information for me."

"Did you and Lucas work together?"

"No. We're focusing on different aspects of linguistics. He began his research in Leeds, and I started in York. We'd get together occasionally for a meal or to compare notes, but Yorkshire is a large county, and we each had our priorities."

Lucas followed the satnav directions, driving northeast past Skipton Castle to the roundabout and war memorial festooned with red poppy wreaths, down a narrow side street, and parked along the curb. "Are you ready?"

Roxanne huffed out a breath. "Yep."

"Hey, Roxy Ruth, do you mind if I sit in the car? I am drained and my joints ache."

"Do you have a fever or the sniffles Are you coming down with the flu?" Nurse Clarke was always alerted by symptoms that could signal a problem.

"No, just sleepy."

"I can sympathize. If the adrenaline left my body right now, I'd collapse in a heap. Let's go, Lucas before I chicken out."

They approached the front door, and he slowed. "Hey, Roxy. I'm glad Avery stayed in the car so I can ask you a question. Has she confided in you? I've been concerned about her for a few months, especially since she returned from Houston. She seems withdrawn and quieter than usual, and she's often tired and complains of aches and pains. Have you noticed she's also losing weight? When I confronted her, she dismissed my concerns."

"She hasn't mentioned anything to me. I've been too focused on my problems to notice but frequent aches and weight loss are often symptoms of something serious. I will ask her."

"Thank you." He cleared his throat and knocked on the door. Seconds stretched into a minute. He knocked again, but no response. "Do you want to leave a note, or call her later this evening or tomorrow?"

"I'll call—"

A woman's voice sounded from the side of the house and then she appeared, carrying two flower pots filled with bright pink begonias. She stopped and asked, "Hello. Can I help you?"

Lucas noted Roxanne hesitate, so he continued the conversation, "Yes. Are you Alicia Maynard?"

"I am not. Who are you?"

He introduced them both and included the reason for their visit. "She's trying to find her mother and Ms. Maynard might have known her."

"Dearie me. We bought the cottage from her and her husband ten years ago."

Roxanne's shoulders drooped. "Do you know where they moved to?"

"No. I never met them."

"Is there anyone else who might know?" Lucas

stepped closer to Roxy.

The woman set down the pots and removed her gardening gloves. "You can ask the real estate agent we used. Richard Grainger has an office on High Street."

"Thank you. Your garden is beautiful." Roxanne turned and walked to the gate.

Back in the sedan, Lucas used his phone and checked the address for the real estate company. When he started the motor, Avery stirred.

"What did you find out, Roxy?" She sat forward and yawned. "Oh, excuse me."

Roxanne explained the situation and then felt Avery's brow. "I'm worried about you."

"No need. I can't wait to get into the hotel room, close the curtains, and snuggle under the duvet."

Lucas glanced at Roxanne. She responded with a nod. "First, we'll ask if the realtor knows where Alicia Maynard moved to, then I promise, we'll check into our hotels."

"Hotels?" Roxanne and Avery asked in unison.

"Busy holiday season. I was fortunate to find three rooms for tonight."

The drive to the realtor's office didn't take long. Avery joined Roxanne and Lucas as they entered the building.

To his surprise, Avery took charge of the conversation. She could be charming in a sophisticated way. Mr. Grainger succumbed to her persuasive spiel and produced the forwarding address for the Maynards which he'd written on the back of his business card.

"As far as I know, they still live there. I send greeting cards to my former clients, and theirs has never been returned."

Roxanne picked up the card from the counter. "Thank you. I've come a long way to find my mother. I hope Mrs. Maynard can help."

Back in the car, Lucas entered the postcode into the satnav. "The house is over forty miles away, on the outskirts of York. How about we visit tomorrow?"

"Sounds good to me." Roxy slipped the card into her purse.

"A good decision, brother."

On the way to the hotel where he'd reserved two rooms, he glanced at Roxy slumped in the seat. "Won't it be great if the first name on our list is the woman in the photo?"

"Yeah." She folded her arms. "But if my mother isn't one of the women named, or if they can't help identify her, then I want to go home. All these twists and turns, highs and lows—as if I've been on every ride at an amusement park—are not good for my mental or physical health. I feel like throwing up."

"Do you want me to pull over?"

"No. It was a fleeting sensation. I'm tired and need to get some sleep."

"Agree. I used up my supply of energy talking to Mr. Grainger," Avery added.

Lucas turned onto a side street and squeezed the

car into the only available spot in the hotel's small lot. He carried Roxann's bags into the lobby, and Avery plodded behind him.

There were several people ahead of them at the reception desk. Ten minutes later, they were given their card keys and headed to the elevator.

A commotion at the desk caught Lucas's attention. Two young boys yelled at each other and almost came to blows before an adult intervened. The man standing behind the family looked familiar. He had curly dark hair, was shorter than Lucas, and wore blue jeans and a red-and-gray striped shirt. Lucas did a double-take. He'd seen the man at the San Antonio airport yesterday. Wearing the same clothes.

The elevator dinged and the doors opened. The man turned and glanced at Lucas. He quickly crossed the lobby and left the hotel.

The hair on the back of Lucas's neck bristled. Was the man following them, or was it a coincidence that he was at the same airport and now the same Skipton hotel? Lucas wouldn't be so concerned if the man hadn't made such a hasty exit.

There was no reason anyone would follow him or Avery, but someone rammed the passenger side of his truck and could have severely injured Roxy, and her apartment had been broken into. Was Mr. Striped Shirt after her?

Avery's room was on the second floor. When she got off the elevator, he gestured for Roxy to follow.

"Let's have a planning session in her room."

He closed the door and set Roxanne's suitcase on the floor. Sitting on one of the single beds, he described the man and the scene he'd witnessed in the lobby.

"Are you sure it was the same man?" Roxanne asked, her voice a little shaky.

"Yes. Unless two men—one in Texas and one in Yorkshire—both have the same ugly shirt. And why did he choose this hotel when there are so many in Skipton?"

"If this man is following us, I wonder if he is connected to Petra? She's the only person I can think of who might want to sabotage my quest."

"Petra would stand out in a crowd, and I didn't see anyone resembling her."

Avery had removed her shoes and lay on her bed. "Roxy Ruth, why don't you share my room?"

The worry line on Roxanne's brow disappeared. "Thank you. I will."

"Good. Okay, Roxy, give me your keycard, please. I'll tell the receptionist we changed our plans. You and Avery will stay in this room, and I'll keep yours. The other hotel is a block down the street. I'll cancel my reservation there and pick up my suitcase on the way back."

He stopped at the door. "Roxy, please don't go anywhere by yourself. If Avery can't accompany you, please text me and I'll be down pronto. Breakfast service ends at nine. Join me at eight, if you like."

Huffing out a deep breath, he headed to the elevator. He'd be extra vigilant and stay awake all night to keep Roxy safe. Or at least have his phone by his bedside. No ugly-shirted man would get near her.

CHAPTER 12

The wheels of a suitcase rattled down the hall past their door. Roxanne stirred as voices accompanied the luggage. She checked the local time on her phone and blinked. Seven forty-five? She groaned and set her feet on the floor. Gaining six hours was messing with her internal clock, but she was ravenous and eager to visit Alicia Maynard.

Dressed in the clothes she'd set out the night before, she tiptoed to the door, but Avery stirred and sat up.

"Where are you going?"

"Sorry. I tried to be quiet."

"You were. I slept well but feel as if I were run over by that train we traveled on. I need my meds."

"Where are they? I'll get them for you." Roxanne had attempted to ask Avery about her health the previous evening.

She'd hesitated, squirmed, and rolled her eyes, and only mentioned fatigue and achy muscles and joints again. Her remedy consisted of over-the-counter pain meds, a heating pad, and drinking herbal tea.

Not satisfied, Roxanne asked if she could examine Avery, and that's when she shoved her pillow over her head to end the inquisition, and mumbled, "I'm too tired. Ask me tomorrow."

Roxanne handed Avery the bottle of medication and a glass of water. "Do you want anything for breakfast?"

"Only yogurt and toast, thanks. I'll make some herbal tea."

After reminding her about continuing their conversation later that morning, Roxanne left the room. Avery had informed her while on the train that hotel rooms in England didn't have individual coffee makers but rather electric kettles, mugs, an assortment of tea bags, instant coffee, and shelf-stable milk in little tubes. Different but okay. She hurried to the dining room and joined Lucas at a table near the window.

"Is Avery coming down?"

"No. She's still tired. I tried to discuss her medical issue but she shut me down by covering her head with a pillow. I'll try again."

"I was tired too, after our long day. She might be more receptive today. Please order and then we can talk more."

Roxanne read the menu the waiter set in front of

her. "What's a Full English?"

"I ordered it."

She looked at his plate, still crowded with bacon, a fried egg, baked beans, and other assorted items. "Interesting, but I'm not that hungry. Um, I'd like the spinach omelet and coffee, please." To Lucas, she said, "Baked beans with bacon and…and mushrooms? Really?"

"Yup. It took a while for Avery and me to appreciate the additions."

The waiter returned with coffee for her and refilled Lucas's mug.

Lucas sipped his steaming brew. "Do you think Avery might be ill?"

"Yes. Considering your concerns, my radar beeped when she refused to answer my questions. I then paid much closer attention to her behavior and appearance. Her face is a little puffy, she shows signs of being depressed, and she uses lotion on her arms frequently."

The waiter set Roxanne's plate in front of her. "This looks and smells delicious." She glanced again at Lucas's plate and pointed to the black disc. "What's that?"

"Black pudding. Want a taste?"

She spread orange marmalade on a piece of toast. "Just a tiny bite. No offense meant, but it doesn't look appetizing."

Lucas placed a small piece on her plate and watched her intently.

She forked the black pudding, placed it in her mouth, chewed it quickly, and then swallowed. She shook her head. "Not a fan. What is it?"

Grinning, Lucas leaned back and folded his arms. "It's also called blood sausage."

"Ugh. No thanks. This omelet is great and all I need."

"Do you have an idea of what might be wrong with Avery?"

"Maybe, but I need to conduct a thorough examination and she must answer my questions. I had a patient last year who developed hypothyroidism and I brushed up on my knowledge of the condition."

Lucas pushed aside his empty plate. "Which means what, exactly?"

"She might have an underactive thyroid."

"What's the treatment?"

"Before we rush into diagnoses and treatment plans, how about I examine Avery first?"

"Of course. Sorry. Concerned brother."

She placed her hand on his arm and squeezed it. "Avery wants yogurt and toast."

"I'll ask our waiter." Lucas signaled the man and placed the order. "By the way, we only had these rooms for one night. Tell Avery we'll check out before driving to York."

The waiter delivered the items on a tray. "Shall I include a pot of jam?"

"Please. She likes strawberry." Lucas placed the

jam beside the rack of toast and carried the tray to the elevator.

Roxanne followed and pushed the up button.

"I wondered why Avery let me make all the arrangements for this trip. I understand now. I wish she'd told me about her aches and pains."

"In my estimation, your plans have been perfectly executed. The only venture I made outside the USA was a little trip to Guatemala with the church youth group. All I had to do was show up."

"Thanks for the compliment." His eyes widened. "It means a lot coming from you. I got a kick out of setting everything in motion. Now, we need to decide our next move. Two of the women live in villages north of Skipton, and one has an address in a village to the east. If we're unsuccessful in the quest, at least you'll see beautiful scenery."

"I texted Tyler last night. Since he knew about the picture, I told him we located the photographer who gave us a lead. I didn't tell him the guy was in Skipton, and Tyler doesn't need to know the names."

"I agree." Lucas walked with her to the room and gave her the tray. "See you in a bit."

Roxanne set the tray on the dresser. She called out to Avery, who was in the bathroom, "Your breakfast is ready. How are you feeling?"

"Better thanks. I'll be out in a jiffy."

She gathered her clothes and repacked her suitcase.

Opening the bathroom door, Avery said, "Thanks.

When we discuss my health, I want Lucas with us."

"I agree. We're checking out this morning." She collected her toiletries from the bathroom.

In between sipping herbal tea and eating her toast and yogurt, Avery packed her belongings.

Ten minutes later, Lucas arrived and carried both their suitcases. He'd already taken his to the car. After the trunk was loaded, he entered the postcode into the satnav. "It says we'll head east and should be there in forty-five minutes."

Avery tapped Roxanne's shoulder. "Okay, friend, you may continue with the questions."

Ideal time. She turned and smiled at Avery and cleared her throat. "First of all, remember I'm your friend, but the nurse in me needs to know more. From my observations and the little you've told me, I think you might have hypothyroidism."

A gasp from the backseat.

"Take a deep breath, Avery. I said 'might'."

"Okay. Please carry on."

"I'll conduct a physical examination if needed." She'd made a list of possible symptoms and removed it from her purse. "After I mention a symptom, think hard and tell me if you've experienced it within the past year. That's a long time, but be as accurate as you can. Three of the symptoms are obvious. Fatigue, joint and muscle aches or pains, and dry skin. I'll check those off."

When Roxanne finished reading the list, she had

check marks beside depression, weight loss, sensitivity to cold, and a puffy face, which might only be discernible to folks who knew her well. Roxanne would check some of the other symptoms during the physical exam.

"One more. Have you ever felt your heart racing, fluttering, or pounding?"

"No. Why?"

"That means you probably don't have an arrhythmia, an irregular heartbeat. Which is great news."

"Okay, then, what's your diagnosis? What's wrong with my thyroid?" Avery's voice cracked.

"I'll give you a brief description, but you must make an appointment with your GP as soon as possible. He—"

"She."

"She will probably refer you to an endocrinologist. Anyway, the thyroid produces hormones that are used throughout the body. Hypothyroidism, which is an underactive thyroid, means it doesn't produce enough hormones. Over time, this...no, I won't go any further. Avery, please, please take my advice seriously. I can't diagnose this condition. It must be confirmed through special blood tests and imaging." Roxanne read the expressions flitting across Avery's face. Surprise, fear, and then acceptance.

Avery huffed out a breath. "Okay, Nurse Clarke, I

will make that appointment when we return home. In the meantime, what should I do?"

"Rest, avoid stressful situations, eat healthy food, exercise in moderation."

"Ha. Stress as in completing a dissertation? Sorry. That just slipped out. I'll follow your suggestions." She leaned back and looked out the side window.

Roxanne turned and glanced at Lucas.

He checked the rearview mirror. "Avery, my dear sister, we'll support you in any way we can. Don't hesitate to ask for our help. Okay?"

"Thanks."

The whine of the engine was the only sound in the car for a few miles, and then Avery tapped Lucas's shoulder. "You've been checking the rearview mirror a lot. Is someone following us?"

"I don't think so, but I've kept watch."

The traffic in York slowed their progress, but finally, Lucas parked outside a modern house on Albion Street. A repeat of yesterday. Avery remained in the car and Lucas accompanied Roxanne to the door.

He knocked.

Roxanne's stomach muscles knotted and she fisted her hands.

The door opened and a short, plumpish woman stared at them through thick lenses. "Hello."

Roxanne didn't expect a positive response as the woman had a large nose and an angular jawline that produced a pointy chin. "My name is Roxanne Clarke and I'm looking for Alicia Maynard."

"I'm sorry, luv. She doesn't live here."

Stepping back, Roxanne glanced at Lucas.

He must have read the disappointment on her face, and asked, "Do you know where she moved to, ma'am?"

The woman giggled. "Don't ma'am me, young man. I'm not the Queen. All I know is Mr. Maynard passed away a while ago, and his wife had a stroke last year. She's in a care home."

"Thank you." Roxanne turned to leave but stopped when Lucas asked another question.

"Is the care home in York?"

If she'd been thinking straight, she would have asked, but her brain cells weren't cooperating.

"I think so."

"Great. My friend is trying to locate her mother. We'll check out the homes."

"Good luck. Ta'ra." She closed the door.

The greeting brought a smile to Roxanne's face. "That is such a cute word. Thanks for being persistent. What next?" She walked beside him back to the car.

"Let's find a restaurant for lunch and hope they have good Wi-Fi. We can find out how many care homes are in York and call them."

"Or visit. I assume a care home is the same as a nursing home."

"Correct."

Avery asked for details of the visit as soon as

Roxanne and Lucas were seated in the car.

"Alicia had a stroke and is in a care home. After lunch, we'll check out those in York." Roxanne held her excitement in check. Her quest reminded her of a scavenger hunt. One more clue leading to the prize.

Lucas stopped at a café a few blocks away. They were shown to a booth and given menus. After ordering, Lucas searched online for care homes in the city. He checked the screen and immediately pulled back. "Whoa. There are over fifteen. It might take us more than one afternoon to visit all of them."

"Hold your horses. Mrs. Maynard had a stroke, and yes, we don't know how severe it was or what her physical needs are. But I would assume since she's in a home, she might require rehab services or physical and occupational therapy. Maybe even speech therapy. Can you search for homes that offer those services to narrow down the list?"

"I'll try."

The waitress delivered their orders.

"After we eat. I'm hungry."

"Me, too," Avery said.

Following Lucas's suggestion, Roxanne chose the fish and chips, which she enjoyed, and she was pleased to see Avery eat a substantial meal of chicken and salad. Setting her empty plate aside, she produced a pencil and a small pad from her purse. "When you're finished, Lucas, I'll make a note of the homes you find."

"I'm done. That was great. Okay, here goes." He tapped his phone and said, "Aah. Their websites are included. Great." He whittled down the list to six that provided the necessary services.

"That's much more manageable." Roxanne had written down the names, addresses, phone numbers, and postcodes. "Let's get started." She walked beside Avery toward the car. "Hey, friend, how are you feeling? Should we find a hotel in York and check the care homes tomorrow?"

Avery hadn't participated much in the conversation and had developed a slight limp. She nodded. "Leave me at the hotel, and you two can still visit the homes."

"Okay." Roxanne waited until they were seated in the car and then informed Lucas of the change of plans.

He leaned over the seat to pat her knee. "Avery, I'm so sorry. You should have told me."

"I'm following medical advice. I had a healthy lunch and now I need to rest."

"Okay, so let's find accommodation." It took a while to locate a hotel that had two rooms available.

By the time they had checked into the small hotel north of the city, the drizzle he'd driven through turned into a deluge.

Raindrops pelted the window as if demanding entry. Avery chose the bed by that window and settled under the duvet with her phone in hand. "Roxy Ruth, will you make me a cup of tea, please?"

"Certainly."

"I can't believe I have so many texts. Sorting through them will keep me busy while you're gone."

Lucas knocked and opened the door. "I mentioned previously I'd like to visit a linguistics professor while in York. I emailed her and told her I was in town. However, she's in Wales, but she gave me the name of the person who has accumulated various documents on Yorkshire dialects. He lives near Grassington. I want to visit him when we're in the village."

"I contacted Opal Carr, and she's agreed to meet me. I'll let her know we'll be in the Settle area soon." Avery patted her plump pillow.

"Okay. I hope we'll get to those villages tomorrow. Roxy, we need to leave. Did you bring an umbrella?"

She handed the tea to Avery and shook her head. "I'll use the hood of my jacket."

"Hey, Lucas you'll never guess who texted me. Dr. Nadine Jones. She's in Leeds for a few days and thanked us for sharing our contacts with her. I'll tell her we're in Yorkshire, too."

"Sure, but, um, please don't suggest we meet. Okay?"

"Okay."

Roxanne narrowed her eyes as she passed Lucas in the doorway. Whenever this Nadine person was mentioned, he tugged on the neck of his shirt and seemed to stumble on his words. Soon, she'd ask about Miss Nadine.

They visited four care homes before they were

given a possible nibble. The receptionist reported that Alicia Maynard had been a resident for six months, but then her daughter moved her to Green Grove Care Home in Knaresborough.

Roxanne almost skipped for joy on her way to the parking lot. "At last, we'll find out if Alicia is the woman in the photo." She shook the rain off her jacket before sitting in the car. "How far is this Knares place?"

Setting the windshield wipers to fast, Lucas shrugged. "Not far in miles, but I'm done driving in a strange city in this downpour. I hope you don't mind, but I suggest we go tomorrow. Knaresborough is on the way back to Skipton. If Alicia isn't the woman, then we'll be well on our way to the next location."

"I've waited this long. Another day won't matter. Besides, I want to make sure Avery is okay."

"I hope she rested so we can leave after breakfast."

"Actually, Mr. Dupree, mornings are very busy in nursing homes. Helping residents dress, serving breakfast, and medication delivery. Ten or ten-thirty would be better."

"Thanks for educating me." He stopped at a red light. "Do you want to eat at the hotel tonight, or should we do takeaway?"

"Takeaway sounds good. This back-and-forth makes me feel like a ping-pong ball being batted across the net. First Skipton, then York. Now Knaresborough, and we're only on the first name. At this rate, we'll be here all summer. If that man is really following us, I hope our travels make him dizzy."

She took a quick glance at Lucas. They'd only been in England two days, and his remarkable transformation caught her off guard. He'd just admitted he made all the arrangements for the trip, but that was probably done in private. However, now faced with the need for instant decision-making, he hadn't hesitated once. If this quest had taken place in Texas, Roxanne would have had a hand in planning, if not organizing, the whole event. But here in a country she'd never visited before, she sure appreciated someone else making the big decisions so she could concentrate on finding Emily Anne. She stared out the side window. *Where are you, Mother?*

Lucas stopped at an Italian restaurant with a side window for takeaway orders. The eating area was on a covered patio with a stack of menus on each table. He and Roxanne decided on their choices and took their place in line. After placing their orders, they found a table at the far end of the patio. His phone rang, and he checked the screen. "I have to take this, Roxy."

He stepped away and she studied the people in line. A family with three young children, an elderly couple, and—

Someone tugged on her satchel strap. She grabbed it, but the force of the tug increased, almost pulling her off the bench. Thankful she'd brought her cross-body satchel, she held onto the strap firmly but had to swing her legs over the bench to keep a hold. By now, the purse-snatcher had a handful of her hair as well. She looked over her shoulder. He had curly dark hair and wore a baseball cap low over his forehead.

While they tussled, Roxanne was drawn away from the table. Where was Lucas? She'd had enough and yelled, "Stop. Leave me alone."

"Give me your purse," the thief said through gritted teeth.

The young man in line approached them. "Hey, let go of her bag."

She grabbed the hand that held her strap entangled in her hair and kicked backward, connecting with his knee. His grip eased, but not enough for her to pull away.

Then Lucas appeared. He swung at the man, hitting him on the shoulder.

The thief stumbled backward, dragging Roxanne with him.

Lucas said, "If you want to live another day, forget about her purse."

He did let go but pushed Roxanne and ran down the street.

She braced herself with her right hand and landed on her side in a bed of decorative rocks around a flower bed, but she held onto her satchel.

Lucas took a couple of steps in the direction the guy had run, then looked at Roxanne.

Her needs took precedence. Taking Lucas's offered hands, she stood and removed gravel from the inside of her wrist and rubbed her side.

"Did he hurt you?"

"No. I'm fine."

"Praise the Lord. It's my fault. I shouldn't have left you alone. Is the locket in your purse?"

"Yes, but—"

Their order number was called, and Lucas picked up the food, then set his free arm around her shoulders. Despite her bravado, she needed that reassurance. The rain had eased up but drizzle continued, and she lowered her hood and climbed into the car.

Seated behind the wheel, Lucas asked, "What were you saying about the locket?"

"The enlarged photo is in my bag, but the original is tucked away in my suitcase."

"Smart move." He inserted the key in the ignition but didn't start the engine. "I'm glad you're all right and he didn't get your purse. I was too angry to take much notice of his face, but I think I saw curly dark hair."

"You're right, and he had an American accent."

"Probably the same man we've noted previously. Why is he following us, and why would he need your purse?" Lucas shook his head.

"To get the locket and photo. Oh, and remember, I sent a copy to Petra and told her I found it in a locket. This man might be her fiancé." She frowned. "Hold your horses. If he is her fiancé why would he need the locket too?"

"Because yours is the original and has the ID number on the back."

"He must assume it has a number. Anyway, I'm glad I left the original at the hotel."

"Me too. I have an idea." He took out his phone and made a call. "I'll put it on speaker. Hello, Mr. Saunderson. This is Lucas Dupree. We visited your shop yesterday and asked about a photograph. Has anyone else inquired about the picture?"

"Yes."

"Drat. A man? What did you tell him?"

"An American man. He was anxious to identify the woman because he said it might be his wife's mother. I recognized the photo, but honestly, I've been swamped, and I couldn't remember the ID number, so I didn't give him any information."

"Thank the Lord. And thank you." Lucas ended the call. "That means he, the man, the...stalker, doesn't have the list of names, and that's why he's following us. His mother-in-law? Instead of fiancé, he could be Petra's husband."

"It's possible. She hasn't made any effort to contact me."

Lucas started the engine and looked at Roxanne. "I won't let you out of my sight until we find your mother, Roxy. You're going to get sick of my constant presence."

She smiled at him and opened her mouth but clamped it shut when the meaning of the words she was about to utter hit home. *No, I won't. I'm enjoying your company.*

CHAPTER 13

The hotel's breakfast menu, although limited, satisfied Lucas and Avery, but Roxanne only nibbled on her toast. "Roxy, are you all right?" He wiped his mouth with the napkin.

She shrugged. "Physically, yes, but my stomach's in knots."

"We'll be in Knaresborough in a few hours. Alicia might be your mother."

Avery patted Roxanne's shoulder. "Today is a good day, Roxy Ruth. I've been praying for you and your quest every night."

"Thank you both. Your support is much appreciated."

They left the dining room and carried their cases to the car. With all the luggage stowed, Lucas programmed the satnav for the care home address in Knaresborough.

Following Roxanne's advice, they set off mid-morning and arrived at ten-thirty on the dot. He parked close to the entrance and they walked toward the doors.

"Hey, brother, let Roxanne visit by herself. We don't want to overwhelm Alicia."

"You make a valid point, but I'd like you to come in with me." She bit her bottom lip.

Lucas noted her action, a sure sign she was anxious. "You talk to Alicia, and we'll wait in the reception area."

"Okay."

They entered the facility. He and Avery hung back while Roxanne approached the desk. "I want to visit Alicia Maynard, please."

The receptionist checked the computer and then said, "She's in room thirty-two, hall three. If she's not there, she might be in therapy. Ask at the nurses' station. Please sign in."

Roxanne signed in electronically and received a stick-on name tag. She glanced back at him and Avery before heading down the hall.

Lucas wanted to run after her, but instead, watched until she reached the nurses' station. He sighed and sat beside Avery. "I'm glad you're feeling better, sis."

"Me too, but I will see my doctor as soon we get home. Roxy checked my neck last night and said the swelling might be another sign of thyroid problems." She patted his knee. "You continue to amaze me."

Lucas snorted. "Really?"

"Yeah. Making all these arrangements on the spur of the moment."

"Why did you let me? Because you weren't feeling well, or—"

"Partly, but also, I could tell you were eager to accompany Roxanne, and I thought you two could make the plans together." She nudged him with her elbow. "I know what your goal is. She fights hard against the idea, but I think she still loves you, too."

He stood and walked to the main doors and back. "It is that obvious?"

"Uh-huh, but I won't interfere or try to influence her."

"Yeah. She won't take kindly to any coaxing or suggestions."

A group of visitors entered and stopped at the desk. Their chatter filled the waiting room while Lucas contemplated how to prove to Roxy he was serious.

"Hey, brother, I have a couple of questions. Are you still seeing Demetrius?"

"Once a month."

"Good. I can certainly see the difference in your attitude, demeanor, and self-confidence. How did your therapist help you go from someone who couldn't decide which brand of milk to buy, to this organized whiz-kid who chooses restaurants and makes hotel reservations on the spur of the moment?"

He sniffed. "The five-minute rule. It—"

"What's the five-minute rule?" Roxanne joined

them and sat in an armchair.

He frowned. "That was a quick visit."

"I haven't seen Alicia yet. She's with the physical therapist but should be back in her room soon." She hiked a shoulder. "The five-minute rule?"

Being completely honest and open was the backbone of any good relationship. Lucas would have told Roxy eventually. Why not now? He sat beside Avery and cleared his throat.

"This sounds serious. Has something happened?" Roxanne glanced from him to his sister.

"No. Yes." Avery patted Lucas's knee. "But it's all good, Roxy Ruth."

He leaned forward, set his elbows on his knees, and looked at Roxanne. "At breakfast yesterday, you complimented me on making our plans. Well, I have an admission to make. Almost a year ago, with Avery's encouragement, I found a therapist who could help me with my indecisiveness. Did you know that indecisiveness is a disorder?"

Roxanne shook her head.

"My issues are not severe enough to be considered pathological, but they did negatively impact my daily life." He paused and studied Roxanne's expression. Was she interested and supportive? Or did she consider his seeking help from a therapist a weakness? She kept her gaze on his face, head tilted, and a slight smile.

All positive, which encouraged him to continue. "Demetrius provided strategies to help me in different situations. The five-minute rule is designed for quick decisions. Literally, I set myself a deadline, and of course, our trip creates natural deadlines. It also helps to work on one decision at a time and to limit the choices."

Avery elbowed him. "Way to go, Lucas."

"Why did you decide to see a therapist now?"

"It was time to grow up and get over the browbeaten person my father turned me into. I've, um, prayed about my insecurities and worked hard at being more decisive." Before the deep dive into his psyche could escalate, Lucas said, "Enough about my situation. Roxy, do you think Alicia is back in her room yet?"

Roxanne stood. "Probably, but before I go, I need to say whatever strategies you've used so far have worked. Thank you for telling me. I have wondered about the changes I see in you and I commend you for your perseverance." She took a few steps and then turned. "I don't know what's wrong with me, but I feel very vulnerable and need support. Will one of you come with me, please?"

Avery would be the obvious choice, but she winked at Lucas when he glanced at her.

"I'll accompany you, Roxy." *I'll hold your hand, I'll surround you with reassurance.*

"Thanks, Lucas."

He walked beside her down the hall and turned left into a shorter hall.

"Here's her room." Roxanne knocked on the ajar

door.

"Come." The word was slurred.

They entered and Lucas remained in the background. A woman sat in a wheelchair close to the window. She held an e-reader, which she set down on a lapboard clipped to the chair's right armrest. Her paralyzed arm with twisted fingers rested in her lap and her drooping left eye and slanted mouth were more evidence of her stroke.

"Hello. We're sorry to bother you, but I'm trying to find my mother and you might be able to help me."

The woman nodded and pointed to the small sofa. "Please sit."

Roxy perched on the edge of the seat. "Are you Alicia Maynard?"

"Yes. Why?" She dabbed at saliva that seeped out of the corner of her crooked mouth.

"I want to identify the woman in this photo." Roxy stood and held out the enlarged picture. "Is this you?"

Alicia took the photo, glanced at it, and returned it to Roxanne. "Not me."

"Thank you." Roxanne hurried past Lucas and the rubber soles of her sneakers squeaked on the tile floors.

He smiled at Alicia. "What are you reading?"

Her eyes sparkled. "*Deep Fire*. I love science fiction."

"It's a great story. I hope you enjoy it. Goodbye." He met Avery and Roxanne in the reception area and led the way to the car.

"Another disappointment." Roxanne buckled her seat belt. "I suppose I was naïve to think I'd find my mother quickly." She sighed. "Oh, well. If nothing else, I'll get to see parts of Yorkshire."

"In my opinion, the scenery only gets better the further we drive into the Dales National Park." He was ready to leave the care home parking lot but waited to start the engine. "The address of the next woman on the list is in Grassington, about forty miles away. However, navigating the narrow roads will take extra time."

Although focused on his driving, Lucas glanced at Roxy frequently. She sat with her hands clasped in her lap and looked out the side window. No telling what rumbled through her mind. But he wouldn't pry. If she had something to say, she wouldn't hesitate. And his view of Avery in the rearview mirror satisfied him that she was okay, at least for the present.

They stopped in Skipton for a light lunch, and he searched online for accommodation. There was nothing available in Grassington for that night, but he found a cottage in Settle, the next village on their list, and reserved it for two nights.

"It's a good thing we're flexible and these villages are relatively close to each other. Next stop, Settle."

The calming sound of the engine's hum was broken when Roxanne said, "Everything is so green. I can't get over the vibrant countryside."

"You ain't seen nothing yet." Avery tapped Roxanne's shoulder. "If you think this is captivating, wait until we get closer to the villages."

"What's that brownish stuff that covers some of the hills?"

"Heather. In a few weeks, little pinkish flowers will transform the brown into magnificent patches of color." Lucas pointed to a swath of brown to his left. "In a few miles, we'll see less and less heather. Rolling green fields dotted with sheep and crisscrossed by stone walls in every direction you look."

"Those white blobs are sheep?"

"Yeah. Black-faced Swaledale sheep have black and white speckled legs, and both males and females have curled horns."

"There are so many."

"Yup. More sheep than people in Yorkshire," Avery added from the backseat. "And see those stone walls? They divide the fields and are made without mortar. Some are hundreds of years old."

"I love seeing old structures still in use. So, this is what the Yorkshire Dales look like. I assume a dale is the same as a valley."

"It is. The dale is usually named after the river that runs through it." Lucas slowed as he entered the roundabout and took the exit toward Settle. "The villages we visit will have many houses that were built in the sixteenth or seventeenth century."

"I'm so glad you're driving. I still have issues with depth perception, and these roundabout things would drive me batty."

"You'll get used to them. When Lucas and I were here doing our research, we drove all over North Yorkshire and never once caused an accident."

"That's reassuring, but I prefer to be chauffeured." She chuckled. "Thanks, Lucas."

Lucas had enjoyed giving Roxanne a brief geography lesson that seemed to distract her from the anxiety she experienced earlier. He drove to Halsteads Terrace and parked along the curb close to the house given as Maud Talbot's address.

"Are you coming with us to meet Maud Talbot, Avery?" Roxanne removed her sunglasses and opened her door.

"Yes. I love these terrace houses and I'd like to ask her when it was built."

They exited the car and climbed the five steps up to the path of paving stones that led to the front door.

Avery rang the doorbell.

Back to her straightforward behavior. She must be feeling better.

While they waited, Roxanne folded her arms, then released them and grabbed her satchel strap with both hands.

A young man opened the door, wiping crumbs off his shaggy beard, and said, "Hello. Can I help you?"

"I hope so." Roxanne had the photograph ready. "Does Maud Talbot live here?"

"Yes, but she's away for the weekend. Why are you looking for her?"

Roxanne showed him the picture. "I'm trying to identify this woman. Do you think it's Maud? It was taken many years ago."

He shook his head. "I have no idea. I'm her lodger and only met her six months ago. Come back Monday morning after ten."

"Thank you. Um, here's my business card. If Ms. Talbot's plans change, please ask her to—"

He scanned the card. "She won't call an overseas number."

"I understand. She could email me."

"I can do that for her. Ta-ra." The young man closed the door.

Avery drew Roxanne down the path. "I know that's not the news you wanted, but the wait will give us a reprieve from driving hither and yon, chasing this illusive woman."

"Avery, you have a way of stating the obvious that lightens my mood." Roxanne walked arm-in-arm with her friend.

Lucas unlocked the car doors and waited for Avery and Roxy to enter the vehicle before climbing in. "We can't check into the cottage until four. Since we'll be there for two nights, I suggest we purchase a few groceries. Crisp bread rolls and butter for me. How about you two?"

"Teabags. My tastebuds have changed and I don't like coffee anymore."

"That's good, Avery." Roxanne smiled at her

friend. "Until your diagnosis is confirmed, I recommend you reduce your caffeine intake. I would like fresh fruit, please."

Lucas stopped to allow pedestrians to cross the road. "The cottage is on a narrow side street. I'll park there if I can, and then we can walk to the grocery store. There won't be any parking spots available in the town center."

He found a place to park a block from the cottage. "Hey, sis. Are you ready to come with us? According to the map on my phone, it's a five-minute walk."

"Let's go. I need to stretch my legs."

At the corner, they turned left onto—

"A cobblestone street. Oh, my stars." Roxanne stared at the stones and then at Lucas. "I've seen them in movies but never dreamt I'd walk on one."

Avery chuckled. "I'm pretty sure every village has a few."

Roxanne walked ahead of Lucas and Avery and pointed to the cottage gardens. "And the colorful flowers everywhere, the cool temperatures. So far, I like Settle."

Shoving his hands into his pockets, Lucas couldn't help but smile at Roxy's enthusiasm. It sure booted her recent disappointment down the road.

They purchased their items and stowed them in the reusable shopping bag Avery had in her purse. The many restaurants in the vicinity would provide their meals.

Lucas chose a different route back to the cottage which took them past a church building.

Hands on her hips, Roxanne stopped to read the sign. "They have a service at ten forty-five tomorrow. I'd like to attend. Who will accompany me?"

"I will. You shouldn't go by yourself." Lucas turned to Avery. "Why don't you come, too?"

"Okay."

He'd taken this route so they could stop at the car and collect their suitcases. Laden with all the carry-on bags, he walked behind Avery and Roxanne.

Her phone buzzed, and she checked the screen. "A text from…. Oh, no. It must be Maud's lodger. He says another American has just been to the house and showed him an enlarged copy of the photo. He gave the man the same info he gave us."

"Ask him to describe the American." Lucas anticipated the lodger's answer and kicked at gravel along the sidewalk.

Roanne soon received a reply. "The man was middle-aged, with curly dark hair."

"Your stalker." Lucas slowed and scanned the surroundings. "He's smart. He also had the copy enlarged. We know what he looks like, so keep your eyes peeled."

"I can't believe Petra…" Roxanne shook her head. "I can believe she would stoop to subterfuge. I sent her copies of the photo and the brooch but she didn't share the information she gathered."

When they reached the cottage, Lucas punched the code into the lockbox and retrieved the key. Avery and Roxanne entered while he remained in the doorway. He turned and rechecked the area. He noted nothing suspicious, but the hair on the back of his neck prickled as if a dozen ants marched across it.

CHAPTER 14

The two-bedroom cottage met all of Roxanne's expectations of an old-world home. Thick stone walls, ceiling beams, a grand fireplace in the living room, and a small walled garden in the back filled with flowers and shrubs. The only downside—one bathroom. She and Avery shared bedrooms and bathrooms at hotels during the trip, but this bathroom was small. No. It was tiny with little counter space.

Suddenly, Roxanne was catapulted back to her teen years when she and her sister, Dana, shared a bedroom and a bathroom. By then, her parents had adopted five children of various ages. Adam, as the eldest boy, had his own bedroom, but the other two brothers shared a room. The three boys were given the large bathroom with two sinks and a long counter, and Roxanne and Dana were relegated to the small bathroom at the end of the hall. One sink and little counter space.

Dana, a year younger than Roxanne, spent hours bathing, styling her hair, and trying different makeup brands. In other words, hogging the bathroom and leaving a mess for Roxanne to clean up, which increased the tension between the girls. When she protested to Mother, she was given a lesson in compassion. Mother said that when older children were adopted, they came with the baggage of their past, especially if they were over age two. All children needed to be loved, accepted, and encouraged to fulfill their purpose in life.

Quietly setting her toiletries on one side of the dresser, Roxanne bit her lip. Mother's pep talk helped, but as the years passed, Dana resented Roxanne despite being tall, blonde, and beautiful. Everyone noticed Dana, while short, plain Roxanne was ignored. At least, that's how she felt. Dana often claimed Roxanne received preferential treatment because she was adopted as a baby, and Dana always laughed at her firm plans for a future in the medical profession. She eventually left home at age nineteen, citing Roxanne's bossy behaviors as the reason. Well, she had to take charge when no one else would. Roxanne cringed when she recalled her reaction back then.

No matter how many times she'd apologized, Dana had never acknowledged her communication, which only emphasized her guilt. Roxanne had confessed the sin frequently and prayed for strength to overcome the impulse, but sometimes, the need for action and order won. Neil, the brother closest in age to Dana, kept Roxanne updated on her life.

She sighed and closed the bedroom door as Avery was already asleep. A mug of hot chocolate would help ease her out of her dip into self-pity. The cottage hosts had provided a welcome basket filled with cookies, packets of cocoa, tea bags, and instant coffee, along with a small bottle of milk in the refrigerator.

Lucas left the living room, joined her in the kitchen, and sat at the table while she waited for the kettle to boil.

"Is Avery coming down?"

"No. She's asleep." Roxanne prepared her drink and then sat across from him. "I need to send a brief update text to Tyler and email my folks and siblings."

He stretched his legs under the table. "This is a quaint cottage. I'm sorry I couldn't find one with two bathrooms."

"On such short notice, this is fine, but speaking of the bathroom situation, I just had a flashback of growing up with Dana and sharing a bathroom with her. Thank the Lord we had a large bedroom." She cradled the mug with both hands. "Looking back at that time, I realize we were spoiled. Many kids in foster care would have given anything to be adopted by a loving family. If the worst thing they had to endure was sharing a bathroom, they would have been ecstatic. I'm blessed to be a part of the Clarke family."

"Avery and I are blessed, too. I might not have a

positive relationship with my father, but we lacked for nothing, and Mother made us feel special." He leaned the chair back on two legs. "Whew. No more talk of bathrooms. Have you heard from Dana?"

"No." Roxanne sipped the cocoa. "I don't even have a phone number for her. "When we return home, I'll make a trip to Nevada and try to resolve our problem. *My* problem of being bossy." She looked at Lucas. His eyes always hinted at his emotions. She had to glance away before she acknowledged what she saw. "Do you think I'm bossy?"

He had the nerve to chuckle.

She glared at him but then smiled. "Okay, okay. You call it bossy. I call it taking charge when necessary."

"In all seriousness, I have noticed on this trip that you pretty much accept what Avery and I suggest. Is this the new you?"

She had to reflect for a moment. "I have tried to be less bossy with my friends, but as the lead member of staff at the clinic, the job demands I often have to act quickly and decisively. As for this trip, if it was just a vacation, I would have been involved in the planning. But knowing you and Avery have been here before, I trust you both to take care of business so I can focus on finding Emily Anne."

"Sounds reasonable."

Taking her empty mug to the sink, she rinsed it out and turned to face him. "Speaking of making changes. I am so glad you've been seeing a counselor, and I'm humbled that you shared the information with me. The changes in your behavior are noticeable and suit you well. You still give us choices, and you don't thrust your opinion on us. All signs of...yes, I'll say it. Signs of maturity. I approve."

He hung his head for a second or two and then looked at her as if she was the only woman in the world. Like he did when they dated.

Not ready to revisit those emotions, she pointed to the doorway. "I'll send my messages upstairs. Good night." She hurried up the narrow staircase and entered the bedroom.

Unprepared to evaluate what had happened in the kitchen, Roxanne sent a short text to Tyler and a long email to her parents and siblings. She showered and slipped into bed, exhausted physically and emotionally. Maybe that's why she fell asleep right away and didn't hear a sound all night.

When Roxanne awoke at seven the next morning eager to dress for church, she glanced at Avery's bed. Good. She was up already. Roxanne knocked on the bathroom door, and Lucas called out. She didn't care that she was wearing yoga pants and a long T-shirt, she ran downstairs and checked the living room, the kitchen, and the small laundry room, but no sign of Avery. Next, she ran out into the small garden in the back. Nothing. The longer she searched, the more her heart raced, and the lump in her stomach grew. Avery could have gone for a walk, or she could have been kidnapped by the stalker.

Overdramatic. Roxanne was reacting to their previous encounters with that man. She ran back upstairs and met Lucas emerging from the bathroom. Hair damp and plastered against his head, barefoot, and only wearing jeans. A citrusy scent wafted around him. Must be the soap he used because he never wore aftershave or cologne.

She blinked but couldn't drag her gaze away from his muscular physique. "Um, have you seen Avery? She's not in the house or gardens."

Lucas slipped on his shirt, and his face turned ashen, legitimizing Roxanne's fear that something untoward had happened to Avery.

"It's not like her to wander off. She wouldn't do something to make us worry. Especially after our discussion yesterday." He followed Roxanne into her bedroom.

"Look. Here's her purse, and I found her phone on the floor beside her bed."

"She has no phone, no credit cards, no identification." Deep furrows etched on Lucas's brow. "This is not good. Get dressed and let's go look for her. Okay?"

"Sure."

"I'll walk along the road in the meantime. Lock the door when you leave and meet me on the sidewalk."

Roxanne donned jeans and a salmon-pink T-shirt,

grabbed her jacket, and ran downstairs, locking the door behind her.

"There's no sign of her on that side of the street. I want us to stay together." Lucas took her hand and walked briskly down the street.

The old exciting sensation of her hand in his brought back so many memories. As a young teen, she'd admired him for how he weathered his father's insults, and later, when they dated, she enjoyed the jealous looks other women sent her way. He was good-looking and muscular and tall, but he was also generous, caring, and a Christian. She shook her head. Not the time to be reminiscing.

They searched the gardens over the low walls and what they could see of the cottages' small side gardens. People walked their dogs; vehicles drove slowly through the neighborhood. At the end of the row of cottages, a large expanse of lawn stretched before them. It looked like a playing field with trees and bushes along the perimeter. A big area to search.

Lucas stopped and ran his fingers through his hair. "Is it time to call the police? Or are we jumping to conclusions that Avery was…what? Kidnapped by the stalker?"

"I had the same thought." Wrapping her arms around her middle, Roxanne stepped closer to the field. A turquoise object fluttered among the line of shrubs in the distance. The object grew larger. She covered her left eye so her right would have better vision. The object— "Over there." She pointed and began to run. "It's Avery. She has a turquoise jacket."

Lucas outpaced Roxanne and reached his sister who staggered and grabbed a nearby branch. "Avery, what...what are you doing out here?" He drew her to him and rubbed her arms. "You must be cold."

"Let's get you home before we bug you with more questions." Roxanne couldn't see any physical trauma but noted Avery's unsteady gait.

With their arms around her waist, Roxanne and Lucas escorted her back to the cottage only a few blocks away. Once inside, Roxanne guided her to the sofa and covered her with a throw rug. "Lucas, please make her a cup of herbal tea."

Avery lay back against the cushions. "I don't know what happened."

"It's okay. We'll get you warm, and if you don't mind, I'll examine you, and then we'll figure out how you ended up in that field."

Lucas handed a cup to Avery. "I'm making coffee in the French press. Do you want some?"

"Please." Roxanne sat beside Avery. "Take your time. I need to examine you when you finish your tea. Okay?"

She nodded. "This is good. Thanks, Lucas."

"I wish I could take your temperature."

"Why?"

"To rule out hypothermia."

Lucas set a mug on the side table. "Your coffee,

Roxy. Rentals usually have a first aid kit that might contain a thermometer. I'll check in the kitchen."

"Avery, are you warm enough?" Roxanne tucked the blanket around her legs.

"Yeah."

"Found it." Lucas carried a red box with a white cross on the top. He opened it and removed a thermometer.

"Thanks. I wish the kit also contained a blood pressure cuff and stethoscope." Roxanne removed the thermometer from its little box and ran it across Avery's forehead. "Rats, it's in Celsius. 36.1°"

He used his phone to make the conversion. "That is 96.98°F."

"Is that good or bad?" Avery asked.

"A temp of 95°F or below indicates hypothermia. I know the hot tea and blanket have increased your temperature, so to be safe, when you finish your tea, you need to take a warm bath."

"Yes, Nurse Clarke."

Roxanne felt Avery's pulse, looked at the wall clock, and counted the beats for fifteen seconds. Then multiplied the number by four. "Your pulse is slower than normal. Has a doctor ever made a note of this before?"

"No. Up until now, I've always been in good health. Obviously, I had no idea how serious my recent symptoms were. I thought they were the result of the stress I've been under." She gave Lucas her empty cup.

"I'm ready for that bath, Roxy Ruth."

Roxanne followed her upstairs to the bedroom. "I'll wait right outside the bathroom door."

"Why?"

"Because I want to. Okay?" She sat in the hallway and smiled at Avery as she carried a change of clothes into the bathroom.

Why? To make sure you don't fall asleep. Or blackout.

CHAPTER 15

While reviewing Avery's saga, Roxanne made a mental list of numerous reasons why her usually level-headed friend would wander from the cottage. In the middle of the night. None made any sense. If she didn't provide a logical explanation, Roxanne would have to consider taking Avery to a doctor. In the meantime, she thanked God that they'd found her unscathed.

Ten minutes later, Avery left the bathroom with a towel wrapped around her wet hair. "I noticed a hairdryer in the bottom dresser drawer. Come sit with me."

Roxanne pulled up the duvet on her bed and placed her sleepwear under the pillow, tasks she would normally have done before going downstairs. She sat on the bed, arms folded. Concern for her friend's health filled her heart.

Setting aside the hairdryer, Avery brushed her chin-length black hair and then sat on her bed. "Roxy Ruth, tell me the truth. Did you hold back when describing hypothyroidism in the car? How serious is it?"

"Serious enough that I demand you visit your doctor soon. If you don't, I'll drag you there. Even if your thyroid is fine, you need to find out why you're experiencing these symptoms." Roxanne didn't want to make light of the situation, but she felt a moment of levity was needed.

"Okay. No dragging required." Avery hung her head. "What's the prognosis?"

"If your thyroid is wonky, the medications available will help you to live a long—"

"Wait, wait. What's the worst that can happen?"

Roxanne moved from her bed and sat beside Avery, drawing her into a hug. "My dear friend, listen to me. If left untreated, hypothyroidism can lead to infertility and a precarious existence. Even death." There, she'd laid out all the consequences, hoping the seriousness of the situation would sink in.

A voice from downstairs interrupted the silence in the bedroom.

"I bought breakfast, ladies. Come and get it."

"Toss our discussion out of your mind for now. Let's go." Hand in hand, Roxanne and Avery went down the stairs and into the kitchen.

"Both of you need to keep up your strength. Fresh

fruit, egg and bacon rolls, yogurt, but sad to say, no black pudding." Lucas made a flourishing gesture to the items on the table.

Roxanne giggled. "I'm devastated. My favorite back pudding is missing."

"Thanks, Lucas. You must be the only person here who likes the stuff." Avery opened a container of yogurt.

They enjoyed the meal while talking about everything except finding Roxanne's mother and Avery's health.

But Roxanne couldn't ignore the pressing question any longer. She sat back and asked, "Avery, why, how did you end up outside?"

Avery swallowed the last of her orange juice and rested her elbows on the table. "I couldn't sleep. I was hot and sweaty, which is unusual because, ordinarily, I'm cold. I entered the kitchen, turned on the light, and…" She frowned. "I'm trying hard to recall the details. I filled a glass with water and looked out the kitchen window while I drank. Something caught my attention. Um, a small moving light?"

"As if a person used a flashlight?" Lucas set his elbows on the table and clasped his hands. He lowered his head and looked at her.

She hung her head. "Maybe. I'm sorry. I should have—"

"Don't go down that road. What happened next?" Roxanne glanced at Lucas, hoping he'd get the message to hold his anger and concern in check.

"I don't know why, but I was drawn outside and sat on the bench. The flowers smelled wonderful, and it was so quiet." She ran her finger around the rim of her empty glass and inhaled a deep breath. "A loud meow broke the silence. Don't scold me, Lucas, I searched for the cat."

"Of course you did." Lucas scooted his chair closer to his sister. "You and cats. Roxanne and dogs. I love how you both have a soft spot for them."

Avery smiled for a second. "Bushes rustled to my right and then to my left. The meowing continued, and by now, I was determined to find the cat. It seemed she squeezed through the gate in the back wall, and I followed her." Avery held up a hand to Lucas when he groaned. "I know I shouldn't have left the garden, but my brain was out of order, and I wasn't thinking clearly. It was darker back there because of the canopy of trees, and…and…" Staring at the ceiling, Avery shook her head.

Roxanne placed her hand over Avery's. "Don't omit anything, no matter how trivial you think it might be."

"I can't be certain what happened next. The cat must have run off because the meowing ceased. I was confused and didn't know which direction to take." She cleared her throat.

Lucas poured more juice into Avery's glass.

To Roxanne, it appeared he was trying to hide his

anger, but she noticed the vein pulsing on his temple, the clenched jaw, the fisted hands.

She took a sip. "I was a bit lightheaded—"

"Whoa. Has that happened before?" Why hadn't Avery mentioned this? Why hadn't Roxanne asked?

"Once or twice."

"Avery!" Lucas thumped the table. "Why didn't you tell someone? Me? Roxanne?"

She shrugged.

"I get it." His face reddened. "You didn't want to bother us. Sorry for interrupting."

"I know I acted irresponsibly. Please, let me finish. I was disoriented but kept walking, hoping I was heading back to the cottage. Obviously, I wasn't. I didn't have my phone. I saw no people. No cars driving by."

"So, it could have been early morning." Roxanne calculated how long Avery might have been out in the elements. "You were gone about four or five hours."

"That long? I must have collapsed close to the bushes and fallen asleep."

"Sleeping or did you faint?"

"I didn't faint. I remember feeling very tired and just curled up, staring at the stars. And then it was daylight."

Roxanne squeezed Avery's hand. "Thank you. Your explanation gives me a clearer picture of what might have happened." She took Avery's pulse again. "Your pulse rate is almost back to normal."

"Good, but what do you think happened?" Lucas asked.

"Lightheadedness can be caused by dehydration, low blood sugar, anxiety, stress, plus many other reasons, the most serious being heart issues, which I ruled out when we discussed your symptoms a couple of days ago."

"Well, I've tried to relax and not worry about my research, but I admit to not drinking enough and my appetite has been erratic."

"I also think you may not be getting restful sleep, which can cause fatigue that is more than just being tired."

Avery focused on the twisted napkin in her hands, and when she glanced up, her eyes were glistening. "That is exactly what I feel. I want to sleep for days."

"Roxy, should we take Avery to a doctor or clinic?" Lucas scooted his chair closer to his sister.

Her gaze switched from Avery to Lucas. One almost in tears, the other in full protection mode. Roxanne squared her shoulders and used her most authoritative tone. "Here is Nurse Clarke's conclusion. Since this is the first episode and Avery, if you are sure you didn't black out, then I say no. From your description, I don't think you fainted. But, you must be honest with us about your symptoms, and your brother and I will keep watch over you. Day and night."

"You'd better believe it, kid." Lucas hugged her.

She rested her head on his shoulder. "I will. I don't

want to feel so lost and helpless again." Reaching out to Roxanne, she added, "Thank you, my Roxy Ruth. I'm glad my traveling companion is a nurse, and I'm thankful my brother will watch over me."

Roxanne leaned back in the chair and regarded the twins. Avery closed her eyes, and Lucas looked at Roxanne over his sister's head. The concern she'd seen on his face earlier had been replaced by determination and something else.

She'd seen that look before. His intense gaze seemed to penetrate her outer shell all the way to her core. Talk about hearts fluttering. She was sure hers did, and she liked the sensation.

CHAPTER 16

While Avery took a nap, Roxanne and Lucas discussed plans for the coming week. "I think we should go back home so Avery can visit her doctor." Roxanne kicked off her shoes and drew her legs up onto the sofa.

"I understand the need for my sister to see a specialist, but what about your search for Emily Anne?"

"My friend's health is more important than finding my mother or inheriting from my grandfather." She voiced the thought and believed it, but leaving Yorkshire without checking all the possibilities left a hole in her soul.

"You've come this far, and after visiting Maud, you only have the names of two more women to check. Please don't give up. Besides, we must include Avery in the discussion when she awakes." He walked to the window, pulled aside a delicate, lacy curtain, and looked outside. "Something I'd like to do when she wakes, that is if she's feeling better, is to walk around the town. Settle has so much to offer. It's been a market town since the thirteenth century."

"Thirteenth? That's a long time. I'd like to see it."

Lucas returned to his armchair, frowning and rubbing his chin. "I have an idea that might help Avery get back home safely and allow you to continue your search."

"Which is…?"

He pulled out his phone. "You've heard us mention Dr. Nadine Jones."

"Yeah." Finally, she'd find out about this enigmatic woman.

"Avery and I met her while at Rice University, and she's in Leeds right now. I'll call her and ask when she plans to return home. Maybe Avery can travel with her."

"That would be a perfect solution." *Please, dear God, let Nadine provide the help Avery needs.*

He dialed her number but had to leave a message. "Hey, Nadine. When are you returning to Texas? Avery and I need to ask you a favor. Please call me."

"Short and sweet." Roxanne studied his face and noted a blush color his neck. She wanted to know why but also took the opportunity to lighten the mood. "So, Mr. Dupree. I think Dr. Nadine Jones was an important person in your past."

"What?" Lucas sat on the edge of his chair and

glared at her.

She couldn't hold her serious expression and giggled. "Oh, Lucas. Your face. I wish I'd taken a picture. By the way, I love the shade your neck has turned."

Tossing a cushion her way, he leaned back and rolled his eyes. "You win. Nadine and I dated a few times, but it was never serious." He hesitated. "On my part."

"But not for her. The plot thickens. No wonder you blush when her name is mentioned."

He stood and leaned over her. "Not funny. And I don't blush."

"If you say so. But I think the reddish hue accentuates your eyes."

Still bending over her, he studied her face, and then abruptly left the room.

Whew. She wasn't ready for such a close encounter. Rising slowly, she placed a hand over her heart. *Steady, steady.* When her pulse rate returned to normal, she entered the kitchen and set the kettle to boil. She needed a cup of tea while she checked her messages. Her folks had not responded, but her brother Adam did. He had a week off which he was spending in New Orleans.

> *Hey, kiddo. I'm praying for you and your search. You know my encounter with my birth mother was not a success, but I hope yours meets all your*

expectations.

Adam never embellished his communication with unnecessary words.

Voices drew her to the hallway. The twins descended the stairs, both smiling.

"You look rested, Avery. How are you feeling?"

"Good, thanks. But I'd like a cup of tea."

"Coming right up." Roxanne returned to the kitchen and plugged in the kettle again. "Lucas, tea for you?"

"No, thanks. Sis, let's sit in the living room. Roxy and I have a serious issue to discuss with you."

Avery sat on the sofa. "That sounds ominous."

"Not quite, but you can probably guess."

"Going home?"

"Right. Wait to hear what I, we, think is a solution."

Avery accepted the cup Roxanne handed her and frowned. "Okay."

Roxanne sat beside her, holding her own cup of tea. "Lucas will explain."

"I left a message with Nadine." He perched on the edge of the armchair. "If she's returning to Texas any time soon, I'll ask if you can travel together. That would solve—"

"Perfect. Nurse Clarke will be satisfied that I won't be alone, and you can stay with her while she completes her quest." Avery winked at her brother and then took a sip of her tea.

"However, if Nadine is going to stay in England for a while, then we'll all go home," Roxanne added.

"No, Roxy." Avery grabbed her arm. "You can't quit. Lucas, tell her."

"Sorry, sis, although it pains me to admit, I agree. You can't travel alone, and I won't leave Roxy here by herself."

The sincerity in Lucas's tone warmed Roxanne's heart. "Wait a minute." She set her cup on the coffee table. "We've all overlooked the obvious. The three of us can go home together. You visit your doctor, Avery, and then I'll return on my own. The stalker will probably have given up since he'll have no one to follow, and I can complete my search. Or, he locates Petra's birth mother" She expected Lucas to disagree, but his response surprised her.

"That's not a bad idea, Roxy. However, I will come back with you. End of story."

She chuckled. "I just had a vision of driving in England. On the wrong, pardon me, *other* side of the road, negotiating those roundabouts, missing my exit repeatedly." She drew in a breath. "Thank you, Lucas and the drivers in Yorkshire, thank you."

He grinned. "The roundabouts were a challenge."

"Well, now that we have the travel arrangements settled, I want to go for a walk. What do you think, Lucas?" Avery asked.

"Good idea. We can stop at a café for lunch. Be

watchful for anyone following us or acting suspiciously."

"Okay. I refuse to allow that man to make a hermit out of me. I want to enjoy this town and the weather and scenery." Roxanne picked up her phone from the seat. "And I'll take lots of photos."

Lucas directed them down a side street that led to the town center. Vehicles and people filled the area. A cool breeze stirred the leaves on the trees and the sun shone from a cloudless sky.

"I can't believe how crowded it is." Roxanne aimed her phone at buildings, cottages, narrow, cobble-stoned streets, and flower boxes overflowing with vibrant blooms. "The town is so amazing."

"It is, but in my opinion, Grassington, the next village on our list, is even better. Smaller and quaint." Avery slipped her arm through Lucas's. "The restaurants around here are probably full. Let's check on the next block."

A café in a converted cottage had an available table. Roxanne marveled at the stone fireplace with an arched frame at the far end of the room. "Look at that. There's a table and two chairs in it."

Although busy, the staff were efficient and the food satisfying. Even Avery cleaned her plate.

"Hey, Lucas, can we go home via The Folly?"

"Sure. Let's turn left here."

"What's The Folly?" Roxanne walked ahead and took a picture of the twins.

"It's a beautiful old building that is home to the Museum of North Craven Life. I'm meeting the leader of the historical society who helped me previously. She located someone whose ancestors left detailed journals that include words and phrases unique to North Yorkshire and how they've evolved. See that building?" Avery pointed. "That's the folly. It's closed today, so I'll visit tomorrow after we see Maud, and Lucas can show you around and give you details about the old building."

"It's interesting. Unusual for sure."

Lucas's phone rang, and he checked the screen. "It's Nadine. You need to hear this, sis. Hey, Nadine, we're outside. I'll put you on speaker so Avery can participate." He explained his sister's recent medical scares and her need to get home. "If Avery hasn't told you, we're in Yorkshire helping Roxanne with her research. She's a nurse and won't let Avery travel unaccompanied."

"I'm so sorry to hear this, Avery. How can I help?"

"When do you plan to return to Texas?" Lucas asked.

"My ticket's for Tuesday. Why?"

"Can you delay your departure for a day so you and Avery can travel together? We'll take her to Skipton on Tuesday, you can ride the same train to Manchester, and then fly out Wednesday."

"Wait, Lucas." Avery tapped his shoulder. "There's a train station here in settle."

"I know, but we'll take you to Skipton, nonetheless."

"Listen to your brother, Avery. I'll change my flight and let you know the number so we can travel together."

Avery leaned close to Lucas. "I have a better idea. Since we are inconveniencing you—"

"No, you're not."

"Hush, friend. We're grateful for your willingness to accommodate our plans. Let us make the booking for both of us. Don't object."

"If you insist."

"I do. That way, we can be sure to have adjoining seats." Avery raised her eyebrows and smiled.

"Fine. I'll make this sacrifice but only because Lucas asked." She chuckled and ended the call.

He shoved his phone into his pocket and then tugged at the neck of his T-shirt.

"Oh, brother dear. Nadine is still interested in you." Taking Roxanne's arm, Avery said, "I love to tease him."

"Shame on you."

"If he really objected, he'd put me in my place."

Once back in the cottage. Avery went upstairs to rest, and Roxanne reviewed the photos she'd taken. All these activities were entertaining but Monday morning couldn't come soon enough. Would Maud be her mother?

After her shower that evening, Roxanne pulled

back the duvet on her bed and plugged in her phone to charge, but it dinged indicating she had a message. Avery had gone to bed early so Roxanne hurried into the hallway to check. A long email from her parents. She ran downstairs and sat on the sofa to read it.

They were taking a break in the capital city of Harare, buying supplies for the clinic, and while there, they visited a church a fellow staff member talked about.

How ironic. While showering, Roxanne had reflected upon the bizarre events of their morning that had prevented her from attending the church in Settle.

Her mother described the service they attended. There were many similarities to their home church in Texas, but the sermon was an eye-opener. Mother condensed it. Study, refer to Biblical scholars, pray, and then make your own decision as to what you believe is literal and what is not. No sense arguing over the concepts. Don't base your faith on one or the other. Rather than digging in your heels, take the message or principle from the passage or story and focus on spreading the Word and developing the fruit of the spirit in your life.

When her parents spoke to the pastor after the service, he detected their skepticism and invited them to his home. They studied together, and he convinced them they didn't need to understand Hebrew or Greek or Aramaic to know the Scriptures were literal, except for obvious passages such as the parables. They admitted they'd questioned the concept they were taught many times.

Roxanne stopped reading and paced in the living room. What did they mean? Were they disregarding their beloved pastor's instructions? She continued to read and her mouth gaped at the words.

> *We encourage all our children to study the Bible with new eyes. Believe it all. You don't need to have someone tell you which parts are literal and which are not. Read and enjoy!*

Aware Lucas came down the stairs and stood in the doorway, she still couldn't take her eyes off her phone. *Study with new eyes.* Did her parents expect the kids to disregard what they'd been taught all their lives?

"I noticed the light on and had to make sure my sister wasn't planning another evening excursion."

"Just me, reading an email from my parents."

"Are they okay? By the puzzled expression on your face, I'd say not." He sat beside her.

"I don't know. I think the Central African heat has addled their brains." Roxanne summarized her mother's message.

He didn't respond right away. "Many people believe that only some of the Bible is literal. Not me. Now, of course, it contains different types of writing. Poetry, songs or psalms, parables, apocalyptic as in the Book of Revelation, and several more. Those books and passages offer us lessons on daily life or ways to praise God. With me so far?"

"Yep."

"I'm reminded of Paul's teaching in 2 Timothy 3:16 and 17. 'All Scripture is God-breathed and is useful for teaching, rebuking, correcting and training in righteousness, so that the man of God may be thoroughly equipped for every good work.' Another point to consider is Jesus quoted from the Old Testament. He wouldn't have done that if the passages weren't true."

Leaning forward, he looked at her. "What's running through your mind right now?"

"My parents' admission is a complete surprise to me. You might remember from our discussions when we dated that our pastor always said we couldn't trust modern translations of the Scriptures to be accurate."

"I do remember. He might have overlooked or ignored the fact that many of the scholars who were involved in translations used the original languages as their base. They didn't just produce a different version in modern-day English. And, hear me out, just because he knows the original languages doesn't give him the right to decide what is literal and what is not."

"Ugh." Roxanne groaned. "You are making too much sense, Lucas. When did you get to be so smart?"

He snorted. "Not smart as much as...using common sense."

"Ha. Common sense. I used to think I had it in

abundance." She shook her head. "I have to dwell on this idea." Her soul seemed to weigh heavy in her core. Twenty years of believing something only to have her spiritual world upended.

"I agree you need time to evaluate your parents' admission by yourself."

"But I want you to stay." Maybe he could help her untangle her thoughts. "Which pastor do I believe? My pastor, or the one my folks met in Harare? I am very confused."

"I can sense that. Let me take a different track. What if your pastor has been wrong all these years? What if his *opinion* robbed you and the congregation of believing the whole Bible?"

Covering her face with her hands, she shook her head.

"Have I added to your confusion?"

She nodded and frowned. "I suppose I must do what Mother suggested. Read the Bible with the premise it is all true, and then make up my own mind."

He rose and looked straight into her eyes. "Exactly. Use the intellect God gave you to discern the veracity of the Bible. I'm available if you want to discuss anything else."

His intense gaze nailed her in place. Their arguments while they dated never ended this way. "Thank you. I'll stay down here a while."

"As long as you don't go outside."

She narrowed her eyes at him. "I won't."

CHAPTER 17

Carrying the last of the suitcases to the car, Lucas kept a wary eye out for the stalker. He must know by now they hadn't visited any possible candidates all weekend, but Monday provided another opportunity.

Lucas returned to the cottage, removed the trash from the kitchen, and made sure all their purchases were out of the refrigerator. "You gals ready?"

"Coming." Avery hurried down the stairs. "Hey, do you know what's bothering Roxy? She barely ate anything for breakfast and hasn't said a word all morning. And she has circles under her eyes as if she didn't get much sleep."

"She received an upsetting email from her folks yesterday. Let her tell you in her own time." Did she stay up late to read the New Testament books?

Roxanne entered the kitchen, her backpack slung

over one shoulder. "Let's get to Maud's early so we're there before the stalker. Lucas, can you do some creative driving and lose anyone trying to follow us?"

"Of course. Settle has several side streets with twists and turns."

"Thanks. I have three simple questions for Maud. Did she marry Benton in Texas, did they have a daughter, and if so, when was she born?"

"I'd have the same questions." He locked the front door and returned the key to the lockbox. "Creative driving coming up."

He took fifteen minutes to weave in and out of the neighborhood. Confident no one followed him, he parked along the curb on Halsteads Terrace.

A few minutes later, the lodger stepped out of the front door and noticed Lucas in the car. He stooped at the open window. "Maud's not back yet."

"Thanks for letting us know." The young man continued down the sidewalk, and Lucas frequently checked the rearview mirror. No one loitering, and the only parked vehicles were there when they arrived. Nothing untoward in front of them either.

Halsteads Terrace, a block from the main street through Settle, had little traffic, but Lucas kept an eye on any car that entered the street. A white sedan slowed and stopped along the curb. "Heads up. This might be Maud."

A short, plump woman climbed out of the car carrying a small suitcase and headed up the front steps.

Roxanne opened her car door, but Lucas touched her arm. "Best not to ambush Maud. Let's give her time to enter the house."

"Okay." She waited a couple of minutes. "Who's coming with me this time?"

"You go, Lucas," Avery said.

Biting her bottom lip, Roxanne reached the front door and knocked. It opened almost immediately.

"Hello." Maud's gaze switched from Roxanne to Lucas.

"Are you Maud Talbot?"

The woman nodded.

As in previous meetings, Roxanne introduced herself and held out the photo. "Do you recognize this woman?"

Lucas was not expecting a positive response. Maud's face was the wrong shape and her eyes were too far apart.

Maud didn't take the picture but did give it an intense look. "I don't think so."

They had not heard that response before.

"Why are you looking for her?"

"She might be my mother."

Maud stared at Roxanne, then tilted her head. "Let me see the photo again." This time, she took the picture and studied it. She looked off into the distance and wrinkled her brow. "You know, she does look familiar. And so do you. It's summat about the color of your hair that makes me think I've seen it before. But I'm sorry, I can't remember where. I hear an American accent. Do you live around here?"

Roxanne drew in a breath and shook her head. "I came to find my mother. Where...where do you think you saw her?"

Handing the photo back to Roxy, Maud shrugged. "I'm sorry, I don't know."

"Here's my card. Please email me if you recall anything else about the woman."

"I will, luv."

"And Ms. Talbot, if an American man comes and asks the same question, please consider telling him nothing." Lucas placed his arm around Roxy's shoulders.

"Ooh, a little mystery. If he comes, I'll read his eyes. If they aren't nice and friendly, I'll say nothing."

"Thank you." He walked with Roxy down the path.

"Lucas, why did you say that?"

"A little sabotage in our favor." He stopped and squeezed her shoulder. "Are you still confused?"

"Yes. I need time." She entered the car and buckled her seatbelt.

"Well?" Avery leaned forward. "You don't seem as disappointed this time, Roxy Ruth. What did she say?"

"The woman looks familiar, but Maud can't remember where or when she might have seen her. You'll never guess what your brother did. He told her an American man might come and ask the same question and asked her not to tell him she recognized the woman."

"Good for you."

Lucas scanned the street for the stalker but saw no cars he hadn't noticed previously. "Let's visit The Folly. Avery, is your contact available now?"

"I'll text her."

In the meantime, Lucas drove to the building and found a parking spot up the hill.

"It looks ancient and has lots of windows," Roxanne stated.

"It is. It was built in the late 1600s as a residence, but over the years, it has been offices, a lodging house, a warehouse, and several other commercial enterprises. Now it houses the museum and a great café."

"Opal Carr replied to my text. She'll meet me upstairs in one of the offices at one o'clock. We'll have time for a light lunch."

"We might as well eat at The Folly Coffeehouse." Lucas opened the doors for Avery and Roxanne.

Seated close to the giant stone fireplace, they perused the menu.

"I'm not very hungry, but..." Avery glanced at Roxanne, "I will order a salmon salad. How's that?"

"Good choice." Roxanne nudged her with her elbow.

"Oh, and I must have a ginger beer before I leave. Lucas, please order one for Roxy, too. I want to see her reaction."

"Ginger beer?"

"Yeah. It's non-alcoholic but has a strong ginger bite." Lucas approached the counter to place their order. When he returned, Avery was still talking about ginger beer.

"You can buy it in San Antonio, but it's different. Not everything's better in Texas."

"Ooh, them's fightin' words." Roxy held up her fists in mock jabs.

When their order was delivered, Lucas admitted he wanted to see Roxy's reaction to the soda as well but added a caution, "Just sip the ginger beer. You might choke on a large swallow."

She took a sip, frowned, then tilted her head. "Not bad. It'll take some getting used to."

"I love it." Avery set down her glass and forked a piece of lettuce.

Every table in the café was occupied, and a general hum of conversation surrounded them. Lucas bit into his sandwich, and his heart swelled in his chest. His two favorite women, not counting his mother, were enjoying their meal, joking about the effects of the ginger beer, safe and happy.

A young couple entered and stood at the counter to order. He was tall and playfully slipped his arm around her neck, reminiscent of a chokehold.

Avery gasped and then coughed and coughed.

"Hey, sis are you all right?"

She nodded, but her face paled. "Are you both

finished? I must tell you something I remember about that night. Outside."

"Okay. Roxy, are you done?"

She swallowed the last bite of her quiche. "What's wrong, Avery?"

"Outside." Avery left the room and exited the building.

Lucas took her arm as they walked up the hill.

She stopped and leaned against the building. "The actions of that couple reminded me. The night of my escapade...after I left the garden and wandered through the trees, someone grabbed me from behind, and...and..." She panted as if out of breath.

Lucas held his anger in check and said in a calm tone, "Take your time, sis."

Standing on the other side of Avery, Roxy rubbed her shoulder.

"He held his arm across my throat and—"

"In a choke hold?" To keep from pounding the table, Lucas rubbed his jaw, which ached from tightening.

She nodded. "I might have passed out momentarily."

He hugged her. "Thank God, the man, our stalker for sure, didn't do more than that. He could have really hurt you. Or abducted you. Or..." Releasing her, he stared into her face. "Avery, I'll repeat my prayer. Praise God, you're all right. The alternative is too dreadful to contemplate."

Tears trickled down Avery's cheeks. "I know I said it already, but I'm so sorry I left the house. Goosebumps erupted on my arms at the thought of what could have been."

"In light of this revelation, I think we should all return to Texas. Why risk putting lives in jeopardy while I search for my mother?" Roxy folded her arms.

"No, Roxy Ruth. You must stay. Lucas will keep you safe, and I know you won't put yourself in harm's way."

Roxanne hiked a shoulder. "I'm not sure what to do."

"It's almost one. Avery, we'll accompany you when you meet with Opal. I can show Roxy around the museum while you visit."

"Okay." Avery let out a big sigh. "How did he know I would be outside?" She slipped her left arm through Lucas's. "Come, Roxy, take Lucas's other arm."

There was not enough room on the sidewalk for the trio, so they walked down the narrow street.

Having Roxy in such close proximity sent his senses reeling and he almost missed her narrative.

"What if the stalker was staking out the cottage? Turning on the kitchen light might have scared him off. Was he waiting for the opportunity to enter and do…what?"

"He probably knows we haven't identified, let alone located, the woman in the photo. Maybe he's just trying to scare you off." Lucas kept a more sinister reason to himself. He wouldn't let the stalker anywhere near Roxy or Avery again.

They reentered The Folly and climbed the grand staircase. Sure that Opal and Avery were safe behind closed doors, he escorted Roxy around the exhibits, but his mind was not on the task.

She noticed and said, "I enjoyed learning about carpenter Robert Thompson and his carved mouse signature, but let's sit and wait for Avery. I'm tired, and I don't know about you, but I have so much on my mind and this little venture is not sinking in."

"I agree, but please don't give up. You've come this far, and we only have two more names to investigate."

Roxy stood and paced to the mullioned windows. "I suppose you're right. We need to keep watch out for the stalker. He got the better of us when he attacked Avery, but—"

"That won't happen again. Come, sit, please." She returned to the bench, and her leg brushed against his. It could be his imagination, but Roxy's attitude toward him seemed to have softened more since they'd been in Yorkshire. True, she couldn't avoid his company, but she was pleasant to be around, held meaningful conversations with him, and even asked for his advice.

Lucas squared his shoulders. Demetrius would be proud of him. He hadn't relied on any reminders or strategies to help with decision-making. The process was becoming more natural. Of course, the circumstances helped. Avery let him take control due to her health concerns, and Roxy was not in her usual environment. Whatever the reason, he felt so much more secure in his ability to take on whatever came his way. And Roxy had noticed.

"Last night, I found a Bible among the books on the mantel in the living room. I started with the Old Testament and found so many interesting points in the Book of Genesis." She lay her hand on his forearm. "Thank you for adding your wise words to my folks' message."

"I don't know about wise, but you're welcome."

Avery texted she was ready to leave. Lucas took Roxy's hand and climbed the stairs to the office.

"Was your meeting successful?"

Beaming, Avery held up a cloth bag. "Yes. I have two old journals Opal located. She mentioned them last year but only recently met the owner. I'll mail them back to her after I read them. Would you believe they were written by a friend's great-grandfather? He was a professor and used the newly developed International Phonetic Alphabet to document dialects in North Yorkshire. I know what I'll be doing on the flight home."

Avery's excited chatter filled the car as Lucas drove to Skipton. He glanced in the rearview mirror frequently but didn't notice a vehicle following them. The only hotel he found with vacancies was on the other side of town. No problem. He knew they'd been blessed by finding accommodations at the height of the tourist season. Some places were expensive or off the beaten path, but so far, they'd all been comfortable.

Before going to their rooms, Lucas asked Avery to text Nadine.

"Why don't you, brother?"

"Please."

"Okay. If she's in town already, should we have dinner together?"

"Yeah, and—"

"I want to tell Nadine what symptoms Avery might exhibit. What she needs to be aware of." Roxy grinned at Lucas. "And I want to meet the woman who makes Lucas blush."

He playfully swatted at her shoulder. "I don't blush."

Avery and Roxy entered their room, and he climbed the stairs to the next floor. A quick shower, dressed in his last clean shirt and hair slicked back, he sat on the bed and checked his phone. Nadine had booked into a hotel about a mile away. Avery set their rendezvous for six o'clock. He had time to reflect and opened his small Bible to his favorite scriptures on patience. Although he knew them by heart, he liked to read the words out loud.

The first was Proverbs 14:29. "A patient man has great understanding, but a quick-tempered man displays folly."

Next, he turned to I Corinthians 13, the beautiful passage on love. He read verse 4. "Love is patient, love is kind. It does not envy, it does not boast, it is not proud."

His favorite Scripture, above all, was Psalm 46:10, especially the first phrase. "Be still and know that I am God; I will be exalted among the nations, I will be exalted in the earth."

That truth had kept him sane through many trials with his earthly father. And now he needed to internalize the words again. For Avery's and Nadine's safe trip. For Roxanne's reading of the Scriptures to discover what she's missed. For her quest to find her mother without interference from the stalker. And for him to know the right moment to profess his love for her.

Nadine and Avery dominated the conversation during the evening meal, which suited Lucas. Although they did tease him, he had no reason to be embarrassed. Roxy added her input when the reason for Avery's unexpected return home was discussed.

"My diagnosis of hypothyroidism is tentative, however, even if Avery's doctor has a different diagnosis, here are some of the more obvious symptoms to watch for." Roxy focused her attention on Nadine, who sat across from her. "Fatigue, joint pain, irregular heartbeat, severe headache, and lightheadedness. Make sure she stays hydrated and as relaxed as possible."

"I'll take good care of my friend."

Avery smiled at Lucas. "Thank you for making these arrangements."

"Thank Nadine for agreeing to change her flight."

"No big deal." Nadine leaned close to Avery. "Getting you home to see your doctor was reason enough. Now, folks, if you don't mind, I must return to my hotel to make a few more phone calls."

They walked toward the exit and Lucas stopped at the counter.

"Give me the car keys, please." Avery held out her hand.

"Okay."

Roxy accompanied Avery outside, but Nadine stayed with him.

She waited for him to pay the bill and then said, "A while back you mentioned you'd given your heart to someone. That someone is Roxanne, isn't it?"

He nodded and slipped his credit card back into his wallet. "How did you know?"

"By the way you look at her. As if there's no one else in the room. Your expression softens, and your eyes seem to sparkle. Does she know how you feel?"

"No, but I will tell her soon." Waiting for the right moment. After they'd investigated the last two names. He would never take advantage of her vulnerability.

CHAPTER 18

Standing outside the train station, Lucas hugged Avery and said, "Please text me when you arrive in Manchester."

"I will, you worry wart."

He slipped his arm around Roxy's shoulders.

"Take care, Avery. Please, see your doctor as soon as possible."

"Yes, Nurse Clarke. I'll text you the details."

Shortening his steps to match Roxy's, Lucas pointed to the rolling gray clouds. "Let's drive to Grassington before the rain hits."

A gust of wind agitated the flowers in hanging baskets along the sidewalk. Roxy nabbed a band from her purse and drew her luscious hair into a ponytail. A green band that matched her shirt. The perfect color for her. She stopped at the car and waited for him to open the door.

"We don't have far to go, right?"

"Right. Northwest, and most of the ride through the scenic Dales."

She buckled her seatbelt. "I remember. I still can't get over how many sheep there are."

Roxy said little during the drive except to express delight at the rolling, green hills dotted with sheep.

She asked Lucas to stop several times for photos, which he was happy to do. Nadine's words to him sat close to his heart. But Roxy still had a mission to complete, and his goal could wait.

"The only accommodation I found in Grassington is a one-bedroom, one-bathroom cottage." Lucas glanced at Roxy. "I'll take the sofa."

"We'll see. If it isn't long enough for you, I'll take it."

"The cottage does have a downstairs half-bath and a laundry room. I don't know about you, but I need to do some washing. We can't check in until four, so let's find the next woman on your list."

"The stalker doesn't have the names. Although you didn't notice him following us, he might be good at avoiding your eagle eyes."

He continued to follow the satnav directions to Garrs End Lane and parked as close as he could to the cottage at the end of the row.

Roxy knocked on the door, and a young woman in her teens with many pierced earrings and purple and pink hair greeted them. "Yeah?"

"Does Sibilla Barlow live here?"

The girl shook her head.

"Do you know where she moved to?"

"No. Sorry."

Lucas smiled at her. "Is there anyone here who may be able to help us?"

"We've lived here since I was a kid. Ask the neighbors. I have to go. Bye."

She closed the door, and Lucas stared at Roxanne, eyebrows raised.

"We'll check with the neighbors then." He walked along the narrow lane to the next cottage.

"Sibilla's an interesting name. At least the girl didn't say an American man had already asked about her."

No one answered his knock. "Two more places to try." This time, a burly man opened the door. Curly gray hair covered his head and chin.

"Good morning," Roxy said. "Do you remember Sibilla Barlow? She lived in one of these cottages many years ago."

"I do. She lived in the middle cottage before the present family moved in. Sibilla was a lovely woman." He eyed Roxanne and frowned. "Why are you interested in her?"

Roxanne showed him the photo. "I think this woman is my mother. I'm trying to locate her."

The barrel-chested man squinted at the picture. "That might be Sibilla."

"Do you know where she is now?"

"No, but my mother might. They were good friends."

"Is she here?" Excitement oozed from Roxy's voice.

"No. She volunteers at the National Park Visitor Center."

"I know where that is. Can we talk to her? What's her name?"

"Winifred Roberts and I'm Ted."

"Thank you very much, Ted." Roxanne returned the photo to her satchel and withdrew a business card. "By the way, we're not the only people looking for Sibilla. An American man with dark curly hair is also after her. If he comes here, please let me know. Here's my card."

Lucas nodded at Ted and then placed his arm around Roxy's shoulders and drew her toward the car. She seemed to have accepted this frequent gesture.

She settled in the seat, blew out a deep breath, and smiled at him. "We are getting close. I can feel it in my heart."

He drove around the corner and back into the village center. "I'm parched and hungry. How about we stop for lunch?"

"Can you wait a bit? Please take me to the Visitor Center first. I don't want to delay this conversation."

"Sure. There's a large car park at the center." The lot was almost full, and he found a spot at the far end.

As they walked toward the building, Roxy took his hand. The simple action almost wiped his thoughts from his mind. But he remembered an important caution. "Roxy, one thing you need to take into account. Ted said his mother and Sibilla were friends. He might be about fifty. That would make Winifred close to seventy. There's a good chance they're probably of similar ages. She might not be your mother, but your—"

"Grandmother. You're right. Fiona first mentioned the possibility in San Marcos, but I was so excited about finally finding someone who knew Sibilla that it flew right out of my mind." She bit her bottom lip. "However, if Sibilla is my grandmother, then it's possible she will know where Emily Anne is. Right?"

Lucas squeezed her fingers. "Right. Let's go find Winifred Roberts."

People milled about inside the center's store, checking out the merchandise, or chatting with the staff. Twisting her satchel strap, Roxanne waited her turn to speak to a woman behind the counter. "Good afternoon. I'm looking for Winifred Roberts."

The clerk stared at her and frowned. "Oh, luv, you just missed her. She's on her lunch break but will be back about half past one." She continued to stare.

"Thank you." Roxy stepped away and Lucas followed her outside. "Another wait. I keep thinking I've waited this long, another few hours won't matter." She dropped onto a stone bench. "But it does matter.

The time we've been in Yorkshire continues to feel like an amusement park ride that I'm stuck on and can't get off."

He wrapped his arms around her, and she rested against his chest. Tension seemed to seep out of her body as she relaxed in his embrace.

Her phone pinged. She didn't move, but when it pinged again, she eased out of his arms and checked her phone.

"A text from Maud." Roxy read it and giggled. "She says the American man arrived, and since she didn't like his shifty eyes or pouty, thin lips, she told him nothing."

Lucas grinned, but had to add, "That means he's right on our heels." He pulled her into another hug. "Stay close to me Roxy. I'll keep you safe"

CHAPTER 19

Emotions in turmoil and her heart on a yoyo string, Roxanne gently pushed away from Lucas's rock-solid chest. She relished the security his closeness and his words provided, but before she could surrender to anything more, she had to focus on her immediate priorities—find her mother, solve the inheritance issue once and for all, and return to her patients in San Antonio. Maybe then she could evaluate the new Lucas.

She stood and cleared her throat, hoping her voice wouldn't catch. "What should we do while we wait?"

"How about a change of pace, a break from your amusement park ride? We can walk along the river."

"But the stalker is close."

"Correct. If he followed us, then he went to Garrs End Lane. That teenage girl might have given him the runaround, and with Ted on our side, hopefully, he won't know about Winifred for a while."

"Okay. Your logic makes sense. Lead the way."

"We'll take this unusual path down to the river." He went through a gate and was soon on a narrow path with rock walls on either side.

Her phone pinged and she checked the screen. "How about that? It's a long text from Petra. She says, 'You can count me out. My fiancé, a lawyer, discovered more information about my adoption. He spoke to my birth mother, and she never married Benton. Howard's estate is all yours.' So the stalker has nothing to do with her."

"Then who can he be? This whole situation is getting wild."

"But it also means Benton probably married my mother. Now we have to locate her. But back to our business. How do you know about this place?"

"This is Snake Lane or Sedber Lane. I often came here when in the area doing research. It's such a calming scene."

"I can't get over the walls. Seeing them up close gives me a whole new perspective of their width and strength."

"Many walls have been here for hundreds of years. This path was probably originally a packhorse path."

"And, of course, the green fields on both sides are dotted with the Swaledale sheep."

He chuckled. "Yup. Their wool is course and so the uses for it are limited."

"They are unique." She stopped and turned,

looking in all directions. "This has got to be a quintessential picture of Yorkshire."

"The Yorkshire Dales."

She drew in a deep breath. "Cool, clean air."

"It's invigorating. The path joins Grassington with Linton, a small village across the river."

"And what is this?" They passed an old building made from the same stone.

"An abandoned barn."

As they approached a narrow bridge, Roxanne said, "I hear rushing water."

"This is the Tin Bridge over the River Wharfe, and behold, the Linton Falls. The buildings across the bridge are part of the village."

They stood on the bridge where conversation was drowned out by the rushing water.

Roxanne viewed the falls upstream and downstream and then checked her phone for the umpteenth time.

"We can walk along the river and make our way back around to the Visitor Center." Lucas pointed to the wide embankment.

"No. Please, let's go back up the lane so we'll be there when Winifred arrives."

"I understand."

The return walk up the hill was just as enthralling, dodging other people who gawked as she had done. Roxanne hurried to the center and approached the clerk she'd spoken to previously.

"Winifred hasn't come back yet."

"Thank you." Roxanne exited with Lucas. "I suppose we wait outside again." She slumped onto the bench.

Whenever an older woman entered, Roxanne craned her neck to see if she went behind the counter. Nope.

Roxanne paced a bit, sat again, and sighed so many times she was certain she'd used up all her air. Her phone pinged and she checked the screen. "Hmm. Tyler is asking for an update." She moved closer to Lucas. "I haven't kept up my daily communication with him. I guess I'll be as ambiguous as possible and reveal nothing."

"Good idea."

After another hour passed, Roxanne returned to the store. "Did Winifred come back?"

"No. I'm so sorry. She called to say something important came up and stayed home."

Roxanne stepped out of the shop and groaned. Would she ever find what her heart longed for? She never thought she'd ever feel the need to meet her birth mother, but this sojourn in Yorkshire had brought new desires to the surface.

"Lucas, what now? Go back to Ted? Go back to Texas?" She longed to have his arms around her again, but she didn't want to encourage him or give him the wrong idea. With her emotions in turmoil, she didn't want to make a mistake.

"Go back to Ted. See if his mother is at home. We can still ask her about Sibilla."

"You're right. Sorry for indulging in self-pity. Okay, Garrs End Lane, here we come."

Seated in the car, he hesitated to start the engine. "Do me a favor. Let your hair loose—"

"Why?" He used to love to run his fingers through her long hair.

"Remember the woman in San Marcos said your hair was the same color as Emily Anne's. Even Carol mentioned it. That might be what Maud remembered too. If Winifred knew Sibilla well, then the color of your hair would support your claim to be her granddaughter."

She dared to meet his gaze. His brown eyes sparkled and his thick dark hair had grayed at the sideburns, increasing his attractiveness. Removing the band around her hair, she forced her gaze away. "That's a good idea."

"Breakfast was a long time ago. Are you hungry, or do you want to go straight to Ted Roberts's home?"

"A quick meal sounds good." Her phone buzzed indicating another text. "Hey, a text from Ted." She read his message and felt the blood drain from her face. She grabbed Lucas's arm. "The American man arrived, but Ted didn't tell him about his mother's friendship with Sibilla. Ted added, 'He seemed angry and was abrupt with me. If he keeps asking around, he'll eventually hear about Sibilla. But I've given you a head start. Can you come back here? I have a message from my mother."

Roxanne nudged Lucas's arm. "Food can wait."

"I agree." He drove the short distance to Garrs End Lane, pulling over frequently to allow vehicles coming the opposite direction to pass on the narrow roads. "Watch out for a man sitting in a car anywhere near the row of cottages. Our stalker might be watching for us."

With parking spots limited, Lucas drove up and down several lanes before he found a spot that didn't block the road.

Roxanne scanned the area before getting out of the car. "I know Ted said our stalker had already been to his cottage, but no telling if he's still in the area."

"Yeah. He must know what car I drive." Lucas looked up and down the lane. "All clear. Let's hurry."

He knocked at Ted's door which he opened immediately.

"Come in. Young lady, you certainly have a similar color hair to Sibilla."

Roxanne followed Ted down a narrow hall to a small living room.

"Please sit down. Would you like a cuppa?"

Although tempted by a hot beverage, Roxanne's need for information won the struggle. She sat on the sofa and Lucas settled beside her. "Your mother never returned to the Visitor Center after lunch."

"That's why I asked you back here. When I explained your visit and told Mum about the photo, she turned deathly pale. She gave me this message for you. Sibilla lives in another village not too far from here, but she doesn't have much contact with the outside world."

"Why?" Roxanne clasped her hands together to keep them from shaking.

"Let me tell you everything she said, then you can ask questions. Sibilla nursed her injured daughter for several years. Emily Anne had—"

Roxanne gasped. "Emily Anne. She…"

Slipping his arm around her shoulders, Lucas leaned closer. "I know you're anxious for more details, but let's hear what Ted has to say."

Anxious was too mild a description, but she nodded and pursed her lips.

"I never met her daughter." Ted smoothed his beard. "My mother is with Sibilla now, telling her about your visit and possible link to Emily Anne. If she agrees to see you, she will allow my mother to take you to her cottage, and then you can ask about Emily Anne's injury."

Words stuck in Roxanne's throat and she felt the blood drain from her face. She was so close to meeting Emily Anne that she could taste it.

"As you can tell, Roxanne is overwhelmed by this information. Thank you, Ted, for not sharing too much with the American. He's out to sabotage Roxann's quest to find her mother." Lucas stood. "Roxy, let's get some lunch while we wait to hear from Winifred. Okay?"

She nodded and rose. Lucas taking charge and making all the decisions was still a new concept, but she had to admit, it felt good to let go for a change.

They walked down to the village center, and before they entered a pub, Avery texted Lucas. "She reports the train ride was uneventful, and Nadine has a hotel room next to hers."

"I hope she can arrange an appointment with the doctor very soon."

"We can both remind her and let her know we're keeping tabs."

"Yeah. Inundate her with reminders." He chuckled. "She'll love us for clogging up her phone."

While at the counter perusing the pub's menu, a woman further down stared at Roxanne. She elbowed Lucas. "The woman at the other end of the bar is staring. Is my hair a mess?"

He glanced at Roxanne and then at the woman. "No. Oh, look, she's coming over."

Roxane turned.

"Sorry for staring, luv, but you look so familiar. Do you have family in Grassington?"

How could she possibly answer accurately? "That's why I'm here. To find out."

"Oh, my giddy aunt. I've seen an older version of you, but sorry, I'm bad at names and places. Where are you from?"

"Texas."

"I hope you're successful." She walked out of the

bar but stopped in the doorway and took one last look at Roxanne.

Lucas paid for their order and chose a table near the back of the pub. "I told you your hair color is a clear giveaway."

"I'm all the more eager to meet Winifred." She picked up her glass of water but set it down immediately. "Change the subject. On a personal note, I've been quite content for someone else to make plans and most decisions. Namely you. I suppose because I'm in unfamiliar surroundings and trust you and Avery because you've been here before." The waitress delivered their sandwiches. "Thank you." Seated across from Lucas, Roxanne had a perfect view of his face and she wanted to see his reaction to her observation.

She swallowed her first bite of a bacon butty, and said, "You have surprised me no end, Mr. Dupree. Not only have you been your usual respectful and gentlemanly self that I remember, but you've evolved into this formidable take-charge guy while still giving us, me and Avery, the opportunity to agree with your choices and suggestions or not."

An expression of appreciation covered his face and he turned a lovely shade of red.

"I'll tell you again, I'm impressed, Lucas."

He gulped down his water and then glanced at her for a second before hanging his head. "Thank you. You don't know how much your words mean to me."

Roxanne was more than impressed with how he

handled her praise. She had a whole lot more soul-searching to do before she acted on his changed behavior and her changed attitude toward him.

Chatter from the crowded pub filled the room, but Roxanne and Lucas said no more.

As they left the pub, Lucas pointed ahead. "There's a grocery shop down the road. We need a few items."

"Eating out is fine for a while, but sometimes I crave homemade meals."

Shopping didn't take long, and they left with only one bag of goodies.

A minute later, Ted texted Roxanne again. She read it out loud. "My mother just returned home. She will accompany you to Sibilla's cottage tomorrow at ten o'clock."

To keep from collapsing, Roxanne grabbed Lucas's arm and stopped on the narrow sidewalk. "Another day, or part thereof. A quest initiated six or seven weeks ago is about to come to fruition."

"I'm excited for you, Roxy. These next few hours are going to drag by."

She nodded and blew out a breath. "I'll soon meet my mother or grandmother. We must make sure the stalker doesn't follow us." Roxanne leaned against the wall and closed her eyes. *Please, Lord, watch over us tonight and bless our meeting with Sibilla.*

CHAPTER 20

The sofa in the cottage was indeed too small for Lucas. At least it was comfortable, as Roxy reported that morning. She'd folded her bedding and placed it on a small table under the window. Still basking in her compliments regarding his change, he set their breakfast dishes in the sink and then entered the laundry room to check on the washing machine's progress. As he remembered from his previous visit, the washing cycle took forever.

Footsteps on the flagstone floor alerted him to Roxy's presence.

"I'm ready to go."

"Good. By the way, Avery texted that they were at the airport. Their flight is scheduled to leave in an hour. I'm so thankful Nadine is with her. Now, after your momentous reunion, I'll meet Claude, a man who has information for my research." He opened the front door and scanned left and right. No lone man or any cars parked anywhere along the street. "Ted's place is not far, but I'll take a circuitous route to get there."

"I'll keep watch, too."

Close to ten o'clock, he pulled up outside Ted's cottage. The thinnest person he'd ever seen appeared in the doorway with Ted. Talk about a puff of wind…

Lucas walked with Roxy along the short path.

Towering over the woman, Ted said, "This is my mum, Winifred."

"Good morning." Her deep voice didn't match her physical appearance. "Oh, my, Roxanne, I can see the resemblance. Sibilla will be so happy to meet you."

"I've waited a long time for this moment. Thank you, Winfred." Roxy held out her hand which the woman grasped.

"My silver Mini Cooper is parked around the back. Follow me to Sibilla's cottage."

Roxy hurried to their car with Lucas close on her heels. The drive to Conistone took all of five minutes. Lucas kept watch for a vehicle following them but didn't notice one. He and Winifred parked outside a small cottage near the church building.

He opened Roxy's door.

She climbed out, straightened her blouse, and smoothed her hair. "How do I look?"

"A little nervous."

Swatting his shoulder, she smiled. "Not what I meant."

"I know. You look like a granddaughter any grandmother would be proud to acknowledge." He took her hand and walked toward the front door. She had a vice grip on his, but he didn't mind. He was so thankful to be with her at this moment.

Winifred knocked, turned to them, and smiled. "Sibilla's expecting us."

The thick, wooded door squeaked open, and a frail, gray-haired woman stood on the threshold. Sibilla's beauty hadn't dimmed with age.

"Oh, my." She shook her head and opened her arms. "My dear, you look so much like your mother."

Roxy, only a few inches taller than Sibilla, melted into her embrace, and when she pulled back, tears streaked her cheeks.

"Please come in and sit down. I'm sorry my living room's so small." Sibilla chose a padded rocking chair and adjusted the cushion behind her back.

Winifred sat in an armchair and took yarn and needles out of her bag, and Roxy perched on the small sofa close to Sibilla. Lucas had but one option—to sit beside Roxy. Not that he mined.

She rummaged in her purse for a tissue and swiped at her cheeks. "I'm so glad to meet you. I have so many questions, I don't know where to start."

"Before I tell you about my daughter, I have questions of my own. Why are trying to find your mother?"

Taken aback, Roxy frowned. "Two reasons. First,

my search was initiated when my grandfather, whom I never knew about until seven weeks ago, told me in order to inherit his estate, I had to prove my mother married his son." She swallowed and paused. "Second, after I began to investigate, I realized I did want to know about my birth mother. Until then, I'd been content with my adoptive parents. Now, finding my mother is more important than proving anything to Howard Palmer."

"I see you resemble Emily Anne and have the same color hair, but that's not enough. How can I be certain you are her daughter?"

Roxy leaned back, looked at Lucas, and raised her eyebrows.

Hoping he read her expression correctly, he nodded.

"I...I was born with two toes fused. I will show you the faint scars."

Tears formed in Sibilla's brown eyes and she shook her head. "That's the proof I need. Now you can ask your questions."

Roxy withdrew the photo from her purse and passed it to Sibilla. "Is this you or Emily Anne?"

A large photograph of a woman Lucas assumed was Emily Anne stood on the mantel. She resembled Roxy and he wondered if she'd seen it.

Hand over her mouth, Sibilla gasped. "It's me. Enlarged from the picture in Emily Anne's locket?"

"Yes. That one was so small. Tell me about it,

please."

The woman rocked and closed her eyes. "So long ago. I was forty-seven. My late husband gave me the locket for my birthday. Um, he passed away fifteen years ago."

"I'm sorry."

Sibilla handed the photo back to Roxy. "Thank you, but you didn't come here to hear about my life." She cleared her throat. "Winnie, luv, would you make us tea, please."

"Of course." Winifred set aside her knitting and left the room.

"Let me tell you about my Em. She was born in Haworth—"

"Is her name a salute to the Brontë sisters?"

"Yes. I loved their novels."

"And what about your name?"

"Oh, it's just a name that's been in the family for a very long time. Now, Em was our only child, adored by both of us. She met Benton after we moved to Grassington, back in…1995, and went to Texas with him. She wrote often and I saved her letters. I'll give them to you. Two are very special. The first one described her unusual wedding. A common law marriage." Sibilla shook her head and picked up a photo from her side table, holding it with fingers gnarled by arthritis. "It sounded so strange, but she was okay with it. Here's a picture of her and Benton and some friends at the celebration."

Roxy stared at the photo and ran her finger over her mother's image. "She was so beautiful."

Lucas leaned closer and looked at the picture. "She was. You might have Benton's eyes, but the rest is your mother."

"When did she get married?"

"The letter stated the ceremony took place on July 26, 1995. We were concerned because she'd only known him a short time. But she seemed to be happy with Benton and they were going to apply to have her tourist visa extended."

Winifred entered the room, carrying a tray laden with cups, plates, and a teapot. Lucas rose and took it from her, and deposited it on the coffee table. She poured milk into four cups and then added the deep amber-colored tea. "Sugar for anyone?"

"Please." Roxy took the cup offered to her and added a spoonful of sugar.

Winifred handed out cups to Sibilla and Lucas and set hers on her side table.

"Thank you, dear friend. You make the best tea." Sibilla sipped her drink and held onto the cup and saucer as she continued her story. "The other important letter is the one detailing your birth. My Em—"

"Oh, dear Lord." Roxy grabbed Lucas's hand and squeezed. "How could I live for twenty-eight years and not know I craved this information?"

He couldn't move any closer to her if he tried, but he returned her squeeze and whispered, "You're doing well, Roxy."

Without skipping a beat, Sibilla continued as if reading from a script. "During her pregnancy, Benton's behavior had changed, probably due to his drinking. When they met, he never got drunk." Sibilla finished her tea and set down the cup. "Alcohol destroys so many lives. Oh well. Em had an easy pregnancy, but she was in labor for twelve hours. The baby weighed seven pounds nine ounces and had a headful of burgundy-colored hair. Just like she did when she was born. And one more thing,"

Roxy handed her cup to Lucas and scooted off the sofa to kneel at Sibilla's feet. "What else did she say?"

"The baby was born with funny toes. On her left foot. She called them webbed."

Hands clasped together, Roxy gazed at Sibilla. "I had surgery on my toes when I was six months old. I am Emily Anne's daughter."

Sibilla placed her bony hand on Roxy's head. "Yes, my dear. My granddaughter."

Leaning over, Roxy hugged Sibilla and then remained at her feet. "My grandmother."

"Call me Gran."

Chuckling, Roxy said, "Gran. I like that." She returned to the sofa. "Please tell me about my mother."

"Be prepared for some hard truths. Toward the end of her pregnancy, she said they were threatened with dire consequences if they didn't give up the baby. Benton was also blackmailed—"

"What? Why? She gave me up? So she didn't do it voluntarily?" Roxy stood and stepped to the fireplace. "Did Emily Anne elaborate?"

"Yes. Her actions were connected with Benton's past and the death of a friend."

"Was it the same person who threatened her and blackmailed him?" Lucas asked.

"A man named Wesley Palmer. A relative, I suppose."

Mouth agape, Roxy returned to the sofa. "He's our stalker."

"I agree. He's trying to make sure you can't prove your mother married Benton."

"But Howard stated he'd rather give his estate to a charity than let Wesley inherit."

Lucas glanced at Sibilla. "Sorry for waffling on. Wesley is Howard's nephew and Benton's cousin. We're pretty sure he's been following us."

"Well if he comes here, he'll get nothing from me."

"Good. Please continue, Gran." Roxy smiled.

"Em didn't describe how she felt when she gave up the baby two days after birth. She was forced to sign away her parental rights and had nothing good to say about Benton."

"Wait. How could she be forced to do something like that?" Lucas shrugged. "It sounds fishy to me."

"It goes back to the blackmail. Benton was responsible for a friend's death. Wesley witnessed the incident and held the tragedy over Benton's head. He said he had proof, and if the baby wasn't given up, Benton would end up in prison. He also hinted that the life of the baby was in jeopardy."

Her words hung in the room. Roxy stared at Lucas, and he shook his head. One man caused so much pain and suffering.

Sibilla rocked more vigorously. "The following week, Benton told my Em he was leaving. He gave her a large sum of money, and she never saw him again. Since her visa was about to expire, she came back home. We lived in Skipton at the time. I could tell she was devastated by losing you, but we never spoke about it. After a while, she moved to Leeds and focused on her career as a novelist."

"Fascinating. What genre did she write?"

"Historical suspense, she called it. They were good but not my cup of tea."

"Speaking of tea. How about I make another pot? I'll put the kettle on." Winifred took the tray from the room.

"Good idea, luv. There are biscuits in my cake tin."

"Do you have any of her novels?"

"No, but some are still available on that site that's named after a river."

"Amazon?" Lucas had used their site while in England. He'd order Emily Anne's books for Roxy before they returned home.

"That's the one. I included a list of her books in

with the letters." Sibilla shifted in her chair and groaned. "My arthritis is playing up today. Okay, I have a little more to tell you. Em never married again, but I believe she was fulfilled by writing and by knowing you were alive."

Winifred entered carrying a platter of biscuits and little plates, which she handed out and passed around the biscuits.

Lucas was hungry but refrained from taking too many. Three to begin with.

"Ta, luv." Sibilla took a bite of a chocolate biscuit. "I moved here after my husband died and worked cleaning holiday lets. Em visited often, and then in 2015, she was involved in a hit-and-run accident in London. She was only there for a long weekend. Her spine was damaged, she had a broken leg, fractured ribs, and a pierced lung." Sibilla closed her eyes.

"Gran, we can come back another day. You don't have to relive the tragedy all at once."

"No, no, luv. Thank you for considering my emotions, but I must tell you everything now. Obviously, Em had a long recovery. She couldn't take care of herself, let alone work on her stories. She came to live here."

Winifred entered with the tray of tea. She poured cups for everyone and presented the sugar bowl to Roxy.

"Thanks, Winifred."

Sibilla sipped her tea and then dunked a biscuit in

her cup. Popping the soggy treat into her mouth, she rolled her eyes. "I love Romany Creams. Enough dithering. Even after Em recovered, she remained here with me. For safety's sake. She worked from home, writing more novels, and then in 2021 she caught COVID-19. Her immune system was already compromised and she needed specialized care. The hospital in Leeds kept her alive until she was well enough to leave."

The woman stared off into the distance and rocked and rocked as if she were gathering more steam to continue.

Lucas looked at Roxy, whose knee bounced up and down. She'd been given so much family history this morning, and he admired the way she let her grandmother tell the story without unnecessary interruptions.

"I'm almost finished." Sibilla stilled her chair and tented her crooked fingers. "Em might have had a premonition that her time was short. While still in Leeds, she called Benton's lawyer in San Antonio. The man told her Benton had passed away, and when she asked about her daughter, he said he didn't know her whereabouts."

Sibilla blew out a long breath. "My Em came home but passed away a few months later. That's all. Here are all her letters." She presented a box to Roxy. "And here is the photo of their wedding." After giving the picture to Roxy, she leaned back and rocked again.

Winifred approached her and rubbed her shoulder. "I think Sibilla is worn out. She's not been well and needs to rest."

"Oh, I'm sorry. Of course." Roxy stood holding the box as if it contained precious gems. "I don't know how long we'll be in Grassington, but can I come and see you again?"

Sibilla nodded. "And you can ring me. My number is in the box."

"I'd like that. Come, Lucas."

He leaned close and whispered, "What about the brooch?"

"I forgot." She rummaged in her purse, produced the green velvet box, and opened it. "We found this brooch with the locket." Roxy handed it to Sibilla.

She tilted her head and pursed her lips. "Yes. I gave it to Emily Anne before she left. To remember Yorkshire. When she came home she said she didn't know what happened to it."

"Benton must have found it. Would you like to have it back?"

"No, no, luv. You keep it with my blessing."

"Thank you." Roxy returned the small box to her purse. "I'm ready, Lucas." She walked to the door, turned and waved. "Goodbye Gran. I promise I'll call."

"Wait, Roxanne. Come back for a minute, please." Sibilla's voice had grown weaker.

Lucas remained at the open door, and although she whispered, he heard her words.

"We must keep in touch when you go back to Texas."

"Of course. Do you have a landline or a cell phone?"

"I gave you my mobile number."

"We can text each other. Mail letters."

She held out her hands to Roxy. "I'll try. But you must send photos. I can't see the ones on my phone."

"I will."

"Especially of you and your beau."

"Who?"

She jutted her chin toward the door. "Him."

"Lucas?" Roxy stared at him then switched her gaze to Sibilla.

Roxy shook her head.

Sibilla nodded hers. "Yes, luv."

Pivoting sharply, Roxy walked to the door.

CHAPTER 21

Fully aware Lucas heard the last conversation with Sibilla, Roxanne slid into the car, set the box on the floor, and buckled her seatbelt. While he drove down the narrow lane, she looked out the side window. A person on a motorbike going in the opposite direction passed the car.

Thankful Lucas didn't bombard her with comments or questions right away, she huffed out a sigh when they entered Grassington.

"That was an intense session. How are you, Roxy?"

"I don't know." She folded her arms and glanced at him. "Please take me to a quiet, calming place. I need to assimilate all I learned."

"How about the back garden of our cottage?"

She picked up the box and held it close. "I forgot about it."

"Just in case the stalker followed us, I won't drive straight there." Lucas negotiated the crowded, narrow streets and finally parked close to their cottage.

Carrying the box, Roxy walked through the kitchen and out the back door. Trees shaded most of the garden, but the borders of flowers brightened up the small plot. She sat on the wooden bench that faced the small lawn and sifted through the stack of envelopes, holding back her tears. Staring at the photo of her parents, she shook her head. If only…

Lucas joined her and stood in front of the bench. "Do you want me to leave or can I stay?"

"Stay, please."

"Thanks."

"I have such strange emotions bombarding me all at once. I'm relieved we located my birth family but also bewildered by what to do next. Should I tell Tyler so he can inform Howard? Or should I go home and visit my grandfather?"

"I don't think you should tell Tyler anything. How did Wesley know to follow us to England? The only person you told was Tyler."

"Right. Why would he be working with Wesley?"

"After you visit Sibilla again, we should return home and show Howard the proof. You can ask Tyler then."

Roxanne took the list of her mother's novels from the box. "Wow. She wrote fifteen books. I can't wait to purchase one. I want to read everything in here before I see my grandmother again." She crossed her legs and balanced the box on her knee. "I'd love for her to visit Texas, but I wonder if she's well enough to travel."

"Winifred might know."

Returning the list to the box, she sighed. "I'm all mixed up. Sibilla shared so much, but I got the impression she didn't warm to me. In her tiny cottage, I felt closer to Emily Anne than to her. Is it my imagination?"

Lucas set his arm around her shoulders. "I got the same impression. Maybe she was holding back because the narration made her relive her daughter leaving Yorkshire, then giving up her baby, and finally, the accident and her passing."

"Or, she doesn't want to form an attachment to me in case I leave her, too." Roxanne moved closer to Lucas and he pulled her to his chest. His breath fanned her face, surrounding her with care and security. The moment felt so natural she didn't want it to end, but then she remembered his appointment and drew back. "What time are you meeting your guy?"

He checked his watch. "In thirty minutes. Claude texted that he's running late and wants to meet at the Corner Café."

"Thanks for being here for me. I would have been an emotional mess if I had to do this by myself."

Lucas was the first to stand. "I need to check my laundry and get my notebook from my room. See you in a few."

Holding the box with both hands, she stood. Did Lucas give a valid excuse for Sibilla's attitude? Or was Roxanne at fault? Sibilla spoke in a monosyllabic tone most of the time, and she seldom showed any emotion, but that could have been to shield her heart. Yeah, she probably put up a barrier so she could get through the meeting. "Forgive me, Lord, for being insensitive."

Roxanne took the box to the living room and searched for a place to hide it. Since it contained the proof Howard needed, she was taking no chances. Her gaze landed on the large stone fireplace. She removed the fire guard and knelt to look up the chimney. The stonework was rough inside, and she spotted a jagged stone sticking out about two feet up. She balanced the box on the shelf, dusted off her hands, replaced the fire guard, and stood. Yep. A good hiding place.

Lucas ran down the stairs. "Ready?"

"Yes." She removed her phone and sunglasses from her satchel and left the cottage with him. She saw no need to tell him she'd hidden the box. "Will we have far to walk?"

"Nope. The café is on Main Street."

They approached the restaurant and had to jump to the sidewalk to avoid a motorbike and two cars heading toward them.

"I haven't met Claude before. He described himself as elderly, portly, with white hair and a beard. Do you see anyone matching that description?"

Roxanne scanned the diners seated at the tables

outside the restaurant. "Maybe at the last table. He's with a younger woman, but has a stack of books on the table."

"Let's find out." Lucas stood beside the man. "Good afternoon. Are you Claude?"

The man turned and smiled. "I am. Come join me. I haven't had lunch yet, so I'll order in a minute. By the way, I can't drive because of my leg injury. My daughter, Gemma, drove me to my physio appointment."

"And this is my...friend Roxanne."

"I have frequently heard my father's lecture on Old English and Norse influences on our dialect, and I don't want to hear it again." Gemma stood and motioned to Roxanne. "Shall we go for a walk?"

"That'll be great, but I need to get something to drink first."

"We can stop at the grocery shop just down the road."

"See you later, Lucas." Roxanne kept pace with Gemma. Hmm. She hadn't been anywhere without Lucas. She shoved her hands into her pockets and grinned. "Can we go to the river?"

"Certainly. I love walking along the riverbank."

A man carrying a motorbike helmet stood at the next table, talking on his phone. Roxanne glanced at him and he walked away.

After purchasing a bottle of Ribena, a dink Gemma recommended, and a sandwich, Roxanne walked with her companion down a steep road, and then Gemma opened a small wooden gate that led to the vast embankment.

Sheep grazed on the lush grass. Some scattered as they approached, and others raised their heads in disapproval. "These sheep are much bigger than I expected."

"I'm so used to them. We've always raised sheep on our farm."

"Where's your farm, and what happened to your father's leg?"

"Near Hubberholme." She took a bite of her sandwich. "He has nerve damage down his right leg, and he has footdrop. Do you know what that is?"

"I do. I'm a nurse practitioner."

"Interesting. I followed in my father's footsteps and became a teacher."

Clouds dotted the blue sky, and the crisp wind sent a shiver through Roxanne's body. She hadn't thought to bring her jacket. She took a slew of photos, and when Gemma offered to take one of her with the river in the background, of course, she accepted.

After Gemma took the picture, Roxanne pointed to a row of terraced homes overlooking the river. "What a view they must have."

"Yes. They are on Bridge End Road. Such an appropriate name. The one on the end is a holiday let. I believe it has five bedrooms."

"Wow. I'll have to return one day and stay there."

Roxanne gazed across the gently flowing river. That was the first time she'd had any thought concerning her potential inheritance. "Can we go to the Snake Path?'

"One of my favorite walks in Grassington. Have you been here before?"

"Lucas brought me yesterday."

"Let's cross the bridge first and view Linton Falls."

The more photos Roxanne took, the more she was determined to return to the area. In Gemma's company, she relaxed and pretended to be a tourist. Standing on the narrow bridge, she looked upstream and downstream and admired the different falls. Gentle and uniform over a man-made structure, fast and gushing over rocky outcrops. "Such a scenic place."

Gemma drew her phone from her pocket and read the screen. "A text from my father. Ee hah gum. He left a few important documents in the car. I have to get them for him." She turned and ran across the bridge to the grassy bank.

"Wait. I want to…" Momentary fear welded Roxanne in place. Alone, for the first time since… But then she noted the throng of visitors on the bridge. She'd be safe if she stayed, or she could make her way back to the café.

Leaning on the bridge rail, she continued to admire the falls. Suddenly, an arm wrapped around her middle. For a split second, she thought it was Lucas, but then a gruff voice whispered, "Don't make a sound or try to get away."

She turned her head to see her assailant, but his bulky chest prevented her.

The man forced her along the bridge to the Snake Path and into the abandoned barn she'd seen with Lucas. The gloomy, dank interior increased her fear. Repugnant odors indicated animals still frequented the barn. "What do you want? Who are you?" His American accent gave her a pretty good idea that he was her stalker.

He slapped his hand over her mouth and forced her to sit on a rickety chair. "Do what I say or your boyfriend will suffer. Don't yell when I remove my hand." Slipping the strap off his shoulder, he dumped a backpack onto the ground.

"Lucas? What have you done to him?" She couldn't distinguish any facial features as he wore a bandana over the lower part of his face.

He didn't answer, so she asked again. "Hey, where's Lucas?"

"Don't you dare order me about." He fumbled in the backpack, produced a coil of rope, and tied her hands behind her back. With little concern for her bare ankles, he wrapped the rope tightly around them and the chair legs and finally tied a gag in place, a big knot forcing her lips apart.

Reeling from the speed with which her world turned upside down, she took in her surroundings. A small wooden table, a gap in the wall high up, grass or weeds growing where light entered the building.

The man removed something from his backpack, turned quickly, and struck her on the side of her head.

Thank the Lord he didn't use his full strength and that he hit her right side. Her eye was healing but she didn't need trauma close to her corneal transplant. Her environment blurred as blood dripped from the wound into her eye. Mumbling her disapproval did nothing to prod the man to answer her questions.

He returned to the pack, picked up something small, and hid it behind his back as he approached her. Then he cussed and pulled another piece of fabric from his pocket which he used as a blindfold.

Roxanne struggled. Panic rose from her stomach into her throat. She couldn't draw in enough oxygen and she became lightheaded. Her muffled scream echoed in the cavernous room.

He raised the sleeve on her left arm and jabbed something sharp into her deltoid muscle. A shot? Of what?

She wriggled as much as she could in her restraints.

"Quit fidgeting." He reared back and slapped her.

The surprise action shocked her into submission. For the moment.

"If you can be a good little Texan, I'll take off your blindfold and gag. But remember, I have Lucas locked away."

Her body rigid, she nodded. Anything to keep

Lucas from being harmed. Blindfold and gag removed, Roxanne gasped in air. She couldn't see the spot where he'd injected her. "What did you give me?"

"Don't worry. It's only sodium pentothal."

"The notion it's a truth serum is bogus." Rats. Admitting that fact was a mistake. She could have pretended it was working. Was it?

CHAPTER 22

The room spun. From the sodium pentothal or the blow to her head? Roxanne kept her breathing in check. No sense in hyperventilating. Focus. What's he doing? *You must outwit him.*

"The drug is supposed to make you more uninhibited. Here goes. Do you have proof your mother married Benton?"

Clamping her lips together, she glared at him.

"If you don't tell me now, I'll hurt you again. I know about your surgery. How about I hit your left eye?"

"Please don't." If he damaged her eye, she might not be able to have surgery again.

"Okay. I'll just..." He grabbed her shoulders and shook her.

She had no defense against his strength but at least she tightened her muscles to keep from getting whiplash.

"Still not answering? Time to give the pentothal a boost." He opened his backpack and returned with a bottle.

In the dim interior, she couldn't determine any more than that. Acting on instinct, she drew back and almost toppled over.

Standing behind her, he grabbed a handful of hair, tilted her head, and poured a sharp-tasting liquid into her mouth. She couldn't help but swallow some of the alcohol that burnt her mouth. Her neck ached from being stretched, and she couldn't move her head.

Obviously, he wasn't satisfied with how much she swallowed. He pinched her nose. She had to open her mouth, and he poured more alcohol down her throat. Although she choked on every gulp, he didn't stop. It burned as if she drank boiling water, and plenty of it doused her T-shirt.

After he'd emptied the bottle, he stepped away and watched her. He paced, looked at his phone, maybe checking the time. Another turn around the barn, and he sat. "How do you feel?"

She didn't respond. The bottle had pressed her lips against her teeth, and she tasted blood. The faint but distinctive odor of alcohol rose from her shirt. The drink was lacking in flavor, except for a fruity undertone. "What was that? How will it interact with the shodium pento, penthothal?" Not only was she lightheaded, but her words were slurred as well. Having never consumed so much alcohol at once, she assumed she was drunk.

"I have another bottle of vodka. If you don't want to drink it, answer my question." He shook her again and her brain seemed to float out of her head. "Are you Howard's heir?"

She nodded. Words were backlogged in her brain, wanting to escape, but she couldn't get them out of her mouth.

"Do you have tangible proof? If so, where is it?"

She coughed and looked everywhere but at him.

He grabbed her arm and squeezed. "Where?" Then he stormed around the small barn. "What proof do you have?"

She knew she was on dangerous ground. What would happen if he found the letters and the photo and destroyed them? If she couldn't confirm she was the heir, Howard's estate would go to charity.

Cotton filled her mind, but a ton of words were fighting to get out. She wanted to seal her mouth shut, but she couldn't overcome the alcohol's effect. "I have a…letter." Rats. Now, she'd disclosed her secret and she rolled her eyes.

"Where is it?"

She shook her head and muttered, "Mmmm."

"I'll hit you again. Where is it?"

All of a sudden, her brain convinced her mouth to speak. "Okaaay. Don't yell. In the cot…cottage." *Oops*. Her head dropped forward. She had no strength to hold it up. Her heart rate accelerated until she was sure it would take off like a jet engine. She shouldn't have told him, but she had no control of her words now. "Do you…know the addressh?" She giggled. "I think you do."

He grinned at her. "Yup. Thank you so much for doing all the legwork. Your trip to Yorkshire is going to be worthless."

"Wait, wait. I have a queshtion. Oh, my head. It hurts. Um, oh yes. Who are you?"

He snorted. "Wesley Palmer, Howard's nephew."

Giggling again, she stared up at him. "Worth…less nephew."

"He called me that? Well, I'll show him." He slapped Roxanne again.

Her head jerked sideways and her cheek stung. "Ouch. That's not nice. You're mean. Um, have an…import important queshtion. Who gave you…" She frowned. Her thoughts were jumbled, and her words stuck together. "Copy of photo. Where…who gave you?"

"Tyler, my buddy. He also told me you were leaving Texas. I followed you from San Antonio."

Her brain seemed to be swimming in the alcohol and injected chemicals, but she was sober enough to recall Howard's words. A legitimate heir or all his estate would go to a charity. Hmm. Did Wesley know that? She wasn't about to tell him as she had more serious things to worry about. What was he going to do with her?

She didn't have long to wait.

He returned the gag to her mouth and kicked the chair from under her. She fell to the ground onto the stones and vegetation and who knows what else. She turned her head to get her nose away from the rank odors.

He picked up his backpack and headed toward the doorway, then stopped and chuckled. "By the way, I didn't inject you with anything. I just stuck a pin in your arm."

His confession should have given her some relief, but the effects of the alcohol were debilitating. She blinked and shook her head, trying to jolt her brain cells loose. Nothing helped. One second she wanted to sing, the next confusion ruled her brain.

I must get loose. I must get to the cottage before Wesley finds the box of letters. She wriggled her wrists until the rope bit into her skin. "Ouchie, ouchie." She stopped and lay still.

Rustling in the grass outside the doorway caught her attention. A person? A—

Baa. Baa. Baa.

Sheep. All over. Big white sheep. Her befuddled brain tried to make a connection. "Baa, baa, black sheep..." She couldn't remember the next words of the rhyme, but she did remember she needed to escape.

Although her wrists hurt, she twisted them back and forth, back and forth. Finally, the rope loosened enough for her to free one hand. She removed her gag and, forgetting her legs were tied to the chair, tried to sit up. Nope. The room spun more vigorously, and nausea threatened to engulf her.

Voices from people walking past the barn encouraged her, but she had no strength to holler or even whisper.

She had to do something. Aha. Her phone. Despite uncooperative muscles, after several attempts, she pulled it out of her pocket. Would she have a signal in the barn? She aimed the phone in all directions and noticed daylight streaming through the doorway. At least he hadn't locked her in. She giggled. That would be hard to do without a door.

She had a signal. "Amazing Grace... Hush." Her battery was low. Rats. She'd have to make the best of the power she had. Like, make a call. She closed her eyes. "Call...who? I don't know. Um..." Her voice trailed off. "Call 9-1-1? No, no." She wasn't in the USA. Where was she? She scanned the interior. "Oh, yesh, yesh, yesh. Yorkshire." She shouldn't call. Her words wobbled. Text. "Good idea. Text Lucas. Hmm. He's so handsome." *Get busy, Roxanne.*

Phone in her right hand, she held it up to her face. Oops. Could she text with only one hand? She touched the text icon. Aha. What clue could she give him as to her whereabouts?

Details of the place Wesley had taken her were fuzzy. "Yorkshire pudding. Yorkshire...Dales. Barn."

She giggled. "And sheep."

It took several attempts, but she persevered and texted:

I need help meet me in yorkshire dales barn

She dropped the phone, turned on her side, and threw up. "Yuck. Hurry, Lucas."

CHAPTER 23

The meeting with *Professor Claude Fielding* was the highlight of Lucas's research. He'd written the research paper Katherine Kalk mentioned. Not only did Lucas get the details of Old English sounds in the Yorkshire dialect and the impact of the Norse language, but Claude had a dialect map that contained information Lucas hadn't seen previously. He also presented a few old regional newspapers and the oldest book on dialects Lucas had ever seen.

"Claude, I can't—"

Gemma appeared and handed Claude a folder. "There, Da. It had dropped behind the seat."

"Thanks, luv."

Lucas craned his neck to see over the diners at the next table. Expecting Roxy at any moment, he kept his apprehension tethered. "Um, Gemma. Is Roxanne with you?"

"No. I left her at the bridge. She looked like she was having a good time."

His phone beeped. Dadgumit. But he checked anyway. Roxy. He read the text, and before he'd finished, he was out of his seat. "Sorry, Claude. I have to go. This is an emergency. Thanks for the info. I can't take the items right now. Please leave them, along with my package, with the café manager. I'll mail them back to you as soon as I can."

He ran to the cottage, jumped into the car, and drove to the Visitor Center parking lot. Raindrops dotted the pavement. Filling his lungs with air, he ran down the Snake Path, heart thumping and legs pumping. He stood at the barn's doorway. An offkey voice attempted to sing "Silent Night." Was that Roxy? He stepped inside and looked around. She lay in the corner on the dirty floor.

He knelt beside her and took her hand. "Roxy, open your eyes." Her pulse was erratic and there was a sharp odor of alcohol around her.

After untying all the ropes, he lifted her into his arms and carried her up the lane, shouting, "Make way. Make way." Workouts in the gym and practice wrestling bouts were paying dividends. Using his upper body strength and muscular legs made Roxy feel as light as a bag of feathers.

In between groans, she crooned phrases of contemporary songs and hymns. Some were hilarious, and Lucas struggled not to laugh.

The light rain dampened his shirt and Roxy's clothes. He reached the car, opened the door, and set her on the seat. "I'm taking you to a clinic."

"No. No," Roxy yelled.

"Why?"

"Wesley." She hummed and then gasped. "The letter. He knows…gone to cottage. All my fault."

"Do you need a doctor?"

"Nope. Cottage. Hurry. Hurry, Lucas. Hmm. I like…"

"Buckle up." He drove to the cottage. A motorbike lay on the sidewalk, and the front door stood ajar. "Stay in the car, Roxy."

"Okay." She leaned back against the seat. "Stay in car. Stay in car. Why?"

Lucas entered the living room and tread carefully to make no noise. The room was a mess. Cushions on the floor. The drawers in the TV cabinet opened. He should have asked Roxy where she hid the box. Evidently, not in the living room. The kitchen fared no better. Cabinets open, and the contents of drawers spilled on the floor.

Noises from the bedroom caught his attention. He climbed the stairs, aware of every move he made.

Wesley muttered under his breath and his shadow fell across the doorframe. Lucas stood against the wall, poised to attack. Wesley stepped out, and Lucas grabbed him around his middle. He struggled, and Lucas was in no frame of mind to play fair. He threw

Wesley down, straddled him, and twisted his arms behind his back. "Quit fighting me, or I'll put you in a Nelson hold."

With Wesley's submissive body slung over his shoulder, Lucas hurried down the stairs and locked him in the laundry room. He ran outside and carried Roxy to the sofa, ignoring her protest.

"Where's the box?"

"Fireplace. Chimmy thingy." She lay down, moaning and rubbing her head.

He knelt beside the firebox, removed the safety screen, and looked up. "Whew. Praise the Lord, the box is still here. I'll leave it hidden. "

"What's…oh, yes. Letters."

"Are you thirsty, hungry, in pain?"

She frowned. "Wes, Wesley?"

"He's sleeping in the laundry room."

"Funny, Lucas. Thirsty. And, um, he hit me." She gingerly touched the wound and winced. "My cheek. He slapped me. Twice times."

"What a jerk."

"And a very big, ginorm…big headache."

"I'll take care of you, and then call the cops."

"Good. I'm tired."

Lucas ran upstairs and hunted for his bottle of ibuprofen. Back in the kitchen, he poured a glass of water and handed it to Roxy, along with two tablets. "Sip the water, don't take big gulps."

"Nooo gulping."

He'd also located the first aid box in the kitchen and picked up a clean dishtowel, which he'd dampened. He wiped the blood off her face and then placed a large Band-Aid over the small gash along her hairline. There wasn't much he could do for her right cheek. A bruise would show by morning.

"I'll make the call from the kitchen." He dialed 1-0-1, England's equivalent to 9-1-1, non-emergency, and explained the situation. "How soon will you be here? The intruder is not happy with his cell."

He sat beside Roxy. "The police will be here in fifteen minutes."

While they waited, he monitored her breathing, heart rate, and temperature. Normal, as far as he could tell. "How many times did you throw up?" He knew the signs of intoxication all too well. His father was a mean drunk, and he'd watched Mother tend to him time after time.

Holding the glass with both hands, she smiled at him. "Once."

"Are you sure you don't need to go to the clinic?"

"My clinic? Rag something."

"No, a clinic here."

"Uh-uh. You…are all I need. My Lucas."

She leaned on his shoulder, and all his problems seemed to fade away. However, a knock indicated the possible arrival of the cops. "Don't go to sleep, Roxy, and stay upright."

"Okie dokie." She waved to him as he left the

room.

He ushered two police officers into the living room and introduced them to Roxy. "She's the victim. The noise you hear is the intruder pounding on the locked laundry door."

They handcuffed Wesley and then interviewed Roxy, but soon realized she was in no state to answer coherently. The female officer said, "Bring her to the station tomorrow for further questioning."

"Will do. Please let us know what will happen to him." Lucas pointed to Wesley. "I want Roxanne to be safe and free from worry."

"Certainly." The officers left with Wesley.

"Have I been…bad?"

"No. Why do you ask?"

"Cops."

"You were very brave. Now don't think about what happened. Rest, sip your water, and after a bit, I'll make you supper."

"Food, mmm, please."

"Okay." He scrambled eggs for her and made himself a fried egg sandwich. Lunch with Claude seemed like a century ago.

Roxy cleaned her plate, and he filled her glass again. The best remedy for a hangover was hydration and easy-to-digest food.

"Shleep now?"

"Sure. I'll make a palette and sleep on the floor beside the sofa, and get a fresh shirt for you." He poked her in the ribs. "This shirt doesn't smell nice."

She sniffed her shirt and wrinkled her nose. "Yuck." She giggled. "Lucas, Lucas. Lovely Lucas."

"I'll be right back." He gathered pillows, his duvet, and a T-shirt for Roxy. She'd left her opened suitcase outside the bathroom. He dumped the bedding on the floor and tossed the shirt to Roxy. "Do you need help to get to the bathroom?"

She tried to stand. "Maybe."

Arm around her, he walked with her to the half-bath and closed the door. "Holler when you're ready."

In the meantime, he placed her pillow and blanket on the sofa, moved the coffee table out of the way, and set her full glass on the side table.

"Yoo-hoo. Hollering."

Tipsy she may be, but she hadn't lost her sense of humor. He helped her back to the sofa. Not only had she changed shirts, she'd washed her face and reformed her ponytail.

She patted the seat beside her. "Sit, please."

"Okay." He'd never pass up that opportunity.

She drew up her legs and rested on his shoulder.

It wasn't exactly his bedtime, but he'd remain still for as long as he could. He draped the blanket over her.

"Nice."

After dark, Lucas eased up and slipped the pillow under Roxy's head. He made sure her back was against the sofa, and she lay on her side. She hadn't thrown up, but he wasn't taking any chances.

He cleaned up the kitchen, took a quick shower, and texted Avery brief details about Roxy's abduction and Wesley's arrest. She couldn't respond until back in the USA, but he was tired of watching TV and perusing the books on the mantel. Rain drummed on the windows, a serenade to lull him to sleep.

The jabbing in his back grew more intense. Lucas turned over to see Roxy sitting on the edge of the sofa, grinning.

"Good morning, young lady." He sat up and rubbed his eyes. "How do you feel?"

"Embarrassed."

"Why?"

"I've never been drunk before and I have vague recollections of saying strange things."

"That is true, but you have no reason to be embarrassed. You didn't voluntarily drink the vodka."

She rubbed her temples. "Wesley? The box?"

"In jail, I hope, and the box is safe in the chimney. The police want to question you today."

"I must shower first and take something for this headache."

"I need to pick up the material Claude gave me that I left at the café, and then I'll make breakfast. You shouldn't take ibuprofen on an empty stomach."

"I do know that, but thanks for the reminder." She

eased up, stretched, and headed to the staircase

"Do you need help?"

"Showering?"

"No. Up or down the…"

Her laughter cut off his sentence. She was teasing him, and he fell for it. He watched her ascend the stairs and then washed his face in the half-bath and prepared a banana, an apple, and strawberries to accompany the yogurt.

Hair still damp and piled on top of her head, Roxy entered the kitchen and joined him at the table.

He wanted to grab her and spin her around. She found her grandmother. Wesley was out of the picture, and he knew she was warming up to him. What could be better?

"I'll be gone ten minutes max. Save me some yogurt, please." He ran into the village, collected the materials, and ran back.

"I ate all the yogurt."

"I'm crushed, Roxy." With his back to her, he set the materials on the counter with his package on top and then plugged in the kettle.

"Just kidding." She pushed a tub of yogurt across the table.

Instead of coffee, he served hot tea. The host had left a small welcome basket that included teabags, sugar, and a pint of milk.

Roxy's appetite impressed him again, and she drank plenty of liquid. "Your headache might last all day, but keep drinking water, take your meds, and rest. We can visit the police station later in the day."

Squinting, she pointed to the counter. "What's that?"

"A surprise. Did you know there's a bookshop in the village?"

"I did not." Her brows rose. "What have you done?"

He handed her the package.

"It's a book." She tore the paper, looked at the cover, and shrieked. "*The Mistress of Fountains Abbey* by Emily Anne Barlow." Clutching the novel, she stood and kissed Lucas on the cheek. "Oh, you thoughtful man. I have to read it right now." She rubbed her forehead. "Ooh, I shouldn't have yelled and moved so quickly."

"Go and camp on the sofa. I'll clean up the kitchen."

He hummed as he washed the dishes, eager to join Roxy in the living room. Task completed, he stood in the doorway. "Would you like some company?"

"Sure." She patted the seat beside her. "My head's still a bit fuzzy. I'll have to read this later."

She had no idea how cute she looked sitting cross-legged, hair now loose around her shoulders, and her green shirt emphasizing the color of her eyes. Except for the bruise on her cheek and the headache, no one would believe she'd been abducted and forced to drink a quantity of alcohol only yesterday.

"Did you take the ibuprofen?" Is that all he could say? Without discussing plans to find her mother or avoiding the stalker, did they have anything to talk about?

"Right before breakfast." She chuckled. "I woke up about one this morning and took some. You didn't budge."

"We both had traumatic days."

She straightened her legs and scooted closer. "Lucas, thank you for rescuing me."

"Thank *you* for rescuing *me*. I wouldn't have consulted a therapist if not for you."

"I'm thankful you did. I really like this Lucas."

"Enough to marry him?" Dear Lord, the words just slipped out.

Roxy's expression gave no hint as to what her response might be. Answer him? Run from the room? Laugh? And then she tilted her head, and her smile reached her eyes. "Why don't you ask her?"

Whew. He knelt in front of her and took her hand. "I love you, Roxanne Ruth Clarke. Will you be my wife?"

She also got down on one knee, gazed into his eyes, and cradled his face in her hands. Slowly, she drew close and then pulled him toward her and kissed him. Not any old kiss. A deep, passionate kiss that answered his question. She pulled back and said one word, "Yes."

What a fantastic, wonderful, glorious sound.

CHAPTER 24

Two months later:

"Seems like we've been here before." Roxanne slipped her arm through Lucas's and walked beside him to the rental car at Skipton station.

He squeezed her hand. "But I've never been here with my wife."

Happiness, contentment, and joy—which hadn't dissipated since their wedding two days ago—surrounded her, warmed her soul, and promised exciting times in their future.

Lucas stowed the suitcases in the trunk and set the satnav for Grassington where they'd spend part of their honeymoon.

Buckled up and warm, Roxanne removed an envelope of photographs from her purse, a more compact version of what she traveled with in July.

"Avery did a great job of having these printed before we left."

"Sibilla will love them."

Looking through the pictures, Roxanne stopped at one of the wedding party. "Ahh, both our families together. That hasn't happened since we lived next door to each other as kids."

"It was good to see your brothers and Dana. Did you resolve your issues before she returned to Nevada?"

"Sort of. Although she had agreed to be a bridesmaid and will keep in touch, we won't be best friends."

"Your apology was from your heart and she could sense that."

Roxanne closed her eyes. Yes, her apology to her sister was way overdue, and she admitted the part she played in creating the rift between them. "One thing Dana said that hurt but it's what she believed. She called me a bulldozer sister. That's one reason why she left." Roxanne frowned. "However, she added that I'd toned down my bossiness. What do you think?"

"I agree. But why did she think you were bossing her?"

"Not just her, all my siblings. As the eldest of five kids, I felt obligated to help Mother and Dad. And…I like order and consistency."

"Those attributes have served you well in your career."

She thought about the renovation they were planning for Howard's house. "Yeah. I suppose, and will as we create Emily Anne's Camp."

"I can't believe the role Tyler played. Not only did he pass on your texts to Wesley, but he'd mismanaged Howard's finances for years. It's a good thing he couldn't get his mitts on the investments. I hope the forensic accountant can find evidence to lock him up." Lucas took her hand. "Right?"

"Definitely."

"Avery looked good."

"The meds are doing their job to regulate her thyroid. But she's been sneaky. Did you even sense she had a boyfriend in Houston?"

Lucas shook his head. "She must have kept her relationship secret for a reason. Maybe she'll tell you when we're back in Texas."

"I'll certainly ask. I hope she's hired at Rice University. Teaching in-depth courses on phonics will be a perfect job for her." She returned the envelope to her purse. "I noticed you talked to your dad before your folks left."

Staring straight ahead, he didn't say anything for a few seconds which seemed like minutes.

"You don't have to—"

"I want to. Yeah, I finally told him how his degrading speech and actions toward me stunted my emotional growth. He didn't apologize, and I didn't expect him to, but I destroyed the sack of boulders I've been lugging around all these years. I guess the one bright spark was he said he gave up alcohol on their cruise and was going to attend AA meetings."

"That's positive."

"I suppose. He's done it before…"

"Maybe this time it will work." They approached the Wharfe River. And Roxanne rubbed her hands together. "Ooh. We're almost there."

"We're closer than you think."

She glanced at him and then back to the road. They crossed the river, and he slowed and turned right on a narrow lane, Bridge End. The name rang a bell, but before she recalled why, Lucas pulled into the parking area of the first terrace house.

"This is the row of houses I saw when Gemma and I walked along the river."

"Yeah. I remember the picture she took of you. We have the house for five days. Judging by the online photos, it's gorgeous inside, and the view will astound you."

"I can't wait." She climbed out of the car and hesitated. "Front or back?"

"This way." Lucas walked to the back door and removed the key from the lockbox. "Stop right there, Mrs. Dupree." He picked her up and carried her over the threshold. "I've waited a long time to do that."

"Oh, you sweet man." She kissed him, and he set her down. "Wow, wow." She hurried to the living room and stood by the large window that overlooked the garden, the river beyond, and the arched bridge.

"While I'll bring in our luggage, why don't you go upstairs and choose a bedroom."

"Okay." She ran up the stairs. Three bedrooms, only one with a double bed. She removed her jacket, threw it on the bed, and waited for him in the hall.

Lucas whistled as he ascended the stairs. He set the bags down and then glanced in one of the small rooms. "I won't fit in that bed." He repeated the comment after checking out the other small room. He stood in the hallway and set his hands on his hips. "Hmm. There are two beds in the basement and two in the attic. I'd best try them out."

Roxanne grabbed his arm and he gazed at her. His eyes gave his ruse away. "Don't you dare, Mr. Dupree." She pulled him into the large room. "This is *our* bedroom."

During the weeks following their first meeting, the relationship between Roxanne and Sibilla had warmed. Roxanne cherished the letters she sent, each one more affectionate than the last. She had arranged to meet her grandmother at ten that morning. If she agreed, they would take her to their holiday cottage. Roxanne knocked on her door and she opened it immediately.

"Hello, Gran. It's so good to see you again."

Sibilla drew her into a hug. "And you, luv." She

held out her hand to Lucas. "Welcome to the family, young man."

He shook her hand and followed the women into the small living room.

Radiating joy while dancing on cloud nine, Roxanne scanned the room and noticed details she hadn't seen before. Photographs lined up neatly on the mantel, books arranged by height on a shelf, and a glass-fronted cabinet filled with knick-knacks, likely all with their own interesting stories.

"Would you like to visit our cottage?"

"I'm ready to go, child. Lucas, please fetch my green coat from the rack in the corridor."

Coat on, cane in one hand and purse in the other, Sibilla led the way to the car. Roxanne insisted she sit in the front.

When they arrived at Bride End Cottage, Sibilla was enthralled with the place. She walked through each room downstairs, examined the antique pieces of furniture, and then, in the front living room, she gazed out the large window and pointed. "What's that little building at the end of the garden?"

"A summerhouse. Would you like to see the garden?" Roxanne asked.

"Yes, please. I love the roses and begonias. Beautiful."

Lucas assisted Sibilla down the steps and through the garden to the summerhouse.

Carrying the envelope of photos, Roxanne opened

the door.

"Ahh. This is nice. Out of the wind but the sunshine comes in." Sibilla settled in the wicker rocking chair.

"I have pictures of our wedding. Would you like to see them?"

"Of course, child."

Roxanne began with the wedding party photo and named all the participants.

"Five adopted kids. Your parents deserve a medal. What work do they do?"

"Both are doctors. Dad is a general practitioner, and Mother is a gynecologist. They work at a medical mission in Zimbabwe."

"Oh, my."

"They've been there for three years but were able to arrange their furlough now so they could attend our wedding."

Sibilla took her time to look at each photo, sometimes asking for clarification. "Oh, luv. Your rings are exquisite." She pointed to a closeup of their clasped left hands.

"I designed them for us. The small, intertwined vines represent eternity."

Sibilla looked at Lucas and winked. "Good job, young man."

"To earn more credit, I'll put the kettle on." Lucas kissed Roxanne on the forehead. "Be back soon."

She sighed. Thank the Lord they found each other.

"Tea will be most welcome." She pointed to another photograph. "The church where you married is…unique."

"It's certainly not ancient like church buildings around here, nor is it fancy like the abbeys or cathedrals. It's a community church, non-denominational, called Faith and Hope Bible Church. Lucas has attended for a long time, but I only recently became a member." After much study, prayer, and deliberation, she'd made the decision and didn't regret it one bit.

"It's vital for couples to share something so important. You are fortunate. Now, you didn't say much about your grandfather in your letters. Tell me more, please."

The weeks after she returned to Texas were filled with cheerful moments, distressing events, and confusing financial decisions. She thought when she left Yorkshire, her life on amusement park rides would be over. However, her time had been crammed with drama and the rapid developments that had taken over her life. Without Lucas's support, she would have caved weeks ago.

She cleared her throat. "Howard was pleased that I was his legitimate heir. He said I had Benton's eyes. Poor man. I think he regretted the rift between them. He passed away two weeks after we returned to Texas."

"You didn't have much time to get to know him."

"Right. And that also made it difficult to accept his

estate." Difficult for sure. Property, more money than she'd ever dreamed could be hers. Vehicles, farm machinery, and his wife's jewelry. She was still surprised whenever her accountant presented another avenue Howard used as an investment.

Lucas walked across the lawn carrying a laden tray, which he set on the large table close to the summerhouse and poured the tea. He handed Sibilla and Roxanne cups and small plates, then passed around a plate of biscuits and shortbread.

"Grassington has a great bakery." Roxanne held up a biscuit. "Baking is not my forte."

Sibilla chuckled. "Mine, neither."

"However, Lucas is a whiz in the kitchen." Roxanne patted his thigh.

"You are a man of many talents." Sibilla dunked a biscuit and popped it into her mouth. "Did you find out for certain who was blackmailing Benton? I think without that problem, he might have turned out to be a good husband. And father."

"I admit I often played the what-if game." Roxanne rubbed her throat, hoping to massage the lump away. "Emily Anne was correct. Benton's cousin, Wesley, was the blackmailer. She didn't know Benton had a child before me, but he never married her mother. Wesley also threatened that woman and made her give up the baby. He threatened to harm the child and dispose of her body where no one would find it."

Roxanne had to take a deep breath. Retelling the

events as if they pertained to an unknown entity drained her mind and soul. She straightened in her chair. "Wesley had met both mothers, but he didn't know their names, and he never told anyone. It's hard to believe he caused all this heartache so he could share the inheritance. He'd already made Benton promise to divide his father's estate."

Sibilla shook her head and clicked her tongue. "Not an honorable man. I'm glad you inherited everything."

"Yeah. Land, his huge house, investments. I'm embarrassed by my fortune."

"Don't be. What are you going to do now that you've never been able to do?"

CHAPTER 25

What a question! Roxanne hadn't viewed her future with those words in mind, but she and Gran were on the same page. After Howard passed away and the reality started to sink in, Roxanne had a tough time sorting through all the possibilities. She'd eliminated options one by one and finally returned to her first choice.

"I have many plans, Gran." Roxanne hadn't told her about any of them. "First, I resigned from my job at the clinic to fulfill a dream I've had for a while. I want to establish a camp for children and young adults with disabilities, especially Down syndrome. We have plans in the works to renovate and extend the house to include private rooms for campers and their parents or caregivers."

"That's very commendable. I wish I could see it."

Selecting another biscuit from the plate, Lucas placed it on his saucer. "We have many red tape hurdles to jump, but the plans are taking shape."

To check on her gran's well-being, Roxanne assessed her appearance and body language. So far, she seemed to be holding up well. "I'll send photos documenting our progress. By the way, our wedding pictures are yours to keep."

"That's grand, luv. I'll treasure them. I'm not familiar with a camp like that. What exactly will you do for the campers?"

"We plan to include outdoor activities, especially equine therapy and animal-assisted therapy with dogs. I want to choose the dogs from shelters, and we'll have them trained. Build stables and places for the dogs and a clinic for a veterinarian. I'll meet their medical needs, and Lucas will provide speech therapy and physical training. He'll help with the daily running of the camp and has applied to teach linguistic-related courses online."

"That's right. You and your sister are studying languages and dialects." Sibilla smiled. "Who knew our oddities in speech would attract so much interest?"

"Their knowledge led me to Yorkshire." Roxanne glanced at Lucas and then at her gran. "And to you."

"Well then, I'm glad your expertise helped my granddaughter. Now, I have another question. What's happening to your building projects while you're on your honeymoon?"

"My eldest brother, Adam, will oversee the contractors. He was dissatisfied with his job on the oil rigs in the Gulf, so we hired him as our property manager. He's an engineer and has great organizational skills and work ethic."

"That sounds wonderful."

"With your permission, I want to name our endeavor Emily Anne's Camp."

Tears glistened in Sibilla's eyes. "Oh, my dear. That's brilliant." She clasped her hands over her heart. "She would approve."

Roxanne swallowed hard and kept her tears at bay. The chirps of the birds and the wind rustling through the trees were the only sounds in the garden for a minute or so. "Are you warm enough, Gran?"

"Uh-huh. I thought of another question, but it slipped my mind. Oh, well."

"I have a piece of news that might be of interest." Lucas set his cup on the table. "Roxy told you Wesley harassed us and abducted her. Well, he was extradited to Texas. We didn't want to give you any details until we knew his future. He pleaded no contest and is in prison."

"Oh, that is good news." She placed her hand on Roxanne's leg. "I want to talk about your suggestions for my cottage,"

"They are only suggestions, and you won't hurt my feelings if you say no."

"The one problem I have is the cottage is damp and hard to keep warm in the winter."

"Before we leave, we'll organize a contractor for you," Lucas said.

"Wait. Oh, silly me. Winifred's son, Ted, does renovations."

"Great. We'll talk to him."

"That's lovely. I'm very grateful." Sibilla wrapped her arms around her middle. "I am a bit chilly now."

"Me too. Let's walk through the garden to the side gate and the car. Fewer stairs that way."

Lucas loaded the tray, closed the summerhouse door, and returned to the cottage.

When he met them beside the car, he handed Roxanne her jacket. "Thank you, my love. You are very thoughtful."

Sibilla didn't complain about sitting in the front and said nothing during the short drive home. She seemed to rely on her cane more than when she left her home earlier.

"Gran, can we do anything for you?"

"No, thanks luv. I'll sit in my chair and wait for Winifred who's bringing me lunch. I had a lovely time with you and look forward to your letters and more photos."

Before she sat down, she hugged Roxanne and Lucas. "Ta-ra, my dears."

Roxanne hurried out of the cottage and climbed into the car. She wiped her cheeks and sniffed. The results of the reunion far exceeded her expectations. As Lucas drove back to Grassington, she clutched her hand over her heart. She'd left a big piece of it with Gran.

A long walk helped temper Roxanne's muddled

emotions. She'd shared wedding photos with Gran, but she might not see her again. Discussing plans for Emily Anne's Camp reminded her she had no experience running such an enterprise. Lucas clasped her hand, and she smiled at him. At least she'd have dogs. Lots of rescued dogs.

They decided to have lunch at a pub. When they entered, the woman who'd commented on Sibilla's photo during their previous trip to Grassington waved to Roxanne and approached.

"Were you successful?"

"Yes. I'm Sibilla Barlow's granddaughter. Emily Anne was my mother."

"Of course. That's who you resemble." The woman turned to the other customers and yelled, "Ey up." When she had their attention, she added, "Eeh by gum. This is Emily Anne's bairn. All the way from Texas."

Greetings of, "Ey up," and "Ow do?" followed.

"How long will you be in Grassington?"

Roxanne glanced at Lucas, and he placed his arm around her shoulders. "We're spending part of our honeymoon here."

"Congratulations. Ooh, our quiz night is tonight. You must join us. Sometimes we have live music afterward.

"We'd love to." Lucas nudged Roxanne. "I'll be fun."

"Okay."

They had a light lunch and stopped at the grocery shop on the way home. When Roxanne left Yorkshire in July, she began a journal and now spent a few hours updating it to include their wedding, the flight, and Sibilla's visit.

That evening, they returned to the pub and were greeted by cheers of welcome again.

Ted motioned them to his table. "I'd like you to join my team."

"Thanks. We might not be much help." Lucas took off his jacket and hung it on the back of his chair. "I'll get the next round of drinks. Ginger beer, Roxy?"

"Yes, please."

"I don't mean to be judgmental Ted, but I've tried ale and I don't like it."

"No problem. Another pint of bitter for me, and Mum will have a glass of white wine."

"I'll be good to see her again."

"She loves quiz night."

The questions covered a variety of topics. Some were multiple-choice, while others required written answers. Roxanne contributed to a few questions, but she mostly enjoyed the comradery and the conversation, much of which she didn't understand.

They walked arm in arm on their way home. Halfway down the road, they heard sirens wailing through the village.

"Someone's in trouble." Lucas looked over his shoulder. "I don't see flashing lights coming our way."

But the sound grew louder.

When they were close to their cottage, a van sped around the corner. The driver seemed to lose control and headed straight for Lucas and Roxanne. Lucas stepped in front of her. "Watch out!"

That was the last thing she heard before the vehicle swerved but still struck Lucas and slammed into the stone wall. Roxanne tripped over a rock, staggered backward, and landed on her side.

Lucas lay a few feet away. He groaned and shifted to look at her. "Are you hurt?"

"My ankle." She moved her right foot and sucked in a breath. "Not broken, probably sprained. And you?"

"Left arm. Also painful chest."

"Your ribs."

"Maybe." He strained to sit up. "Ooh, that hurt." He placed a hand over his left side. "Do you need help getting up?"

"No, thanks." Once sitting beside him, she said, "Keep your arm as still as possible. Do you feel any blood on your arm?"

"I don't think so." He folded back the cuff of his jacket. "No blood."

"Where does it hurt?"

"Forearm."

"Let me check." She grabbed his elbow and slowly moved her hand down his arm. When he winched, she stopped. "In my opinion, you have a closed fracture, meaning the bones haven't broken through the skin.

Keep it still—"

A police car whizzed past them and stopped behind the van. One office looked inside, and one ran to Roxanne and Lucas.

"Did the van hit you?" The young officer knelt beside them.

They both nodded.

"Are you hurt?"

Again, both nodded.

"I might have a sprained ankle. No broken bones."

The officer frowned.

"I'm a nurse. My…husband has a fractured right forearm and possibly fractured or broken ribs."

"I'll call for an ambulance. Are you okay to wait here for a minute? I need to help my partner."

"How long before the ambulance arrives?"

"A couple of minutes."

"Thanks." Roxanne focused on Lucas. "We're probably going into shock. I'm cold. How about you?'

"A bit, especially since I didn't wear my heavier coat. Do you need my jacket?"

She took his hand. "That's a sweet offer, but…I hear another siren."

The ambulance arrived, and the paramedics evaluated their injuries, tentatively confirming what Roxanne diagnosed—her sprained ankle, and Lucas's fractured arm and ribs.

Much later, Roxanne sat beside Lucas in the hospital waiting room. "We're blessed to have Ted as a friend."

Lucas rested his head against the chair. "Hmm. He'll be here soon to take us home. I can't keep my eyes open."

"The pain meds. I've never broken a bone, but I've witnessed closed reduction before. The orthopedic docs are miracle workers. Aligning bones without surgery. How long will you wear the cast?"

"Four to six weeks."

"And your ribs?"

"Ha. Ooh, I shouldn't laugh. Pain killers, anti-inflammatories, rest, ice."

"Almost the same for me. RICE. Rest, ice, compression, and elevation."

"What a pair we make." He put his good arm around her shoulders. "Well, Mrs. Dupree, this is not exactly what I planned for our honeymoon."

"At least we're staying in a fabulous holiday let and we were able to visit Gran."

"Yup. When we get home, I'll build a fire. We can cozy up on the sofa."

"That's the best decision you've made all day."

"I disagree, my love. The best decision I have ever made was asking you to marry me."

She kissed him, drew back, gazed into his warm brown eyes, and said, "I praise God you are in my life to keep me grounded. I don't want anyone ever to call me a bulldozer again."

VALERIE MASSEY GOREE

THE END

Dear Reader:

Writing this story brought me so much joy. I relived my trip to Yorkshire, to Settle, and to Grassington. I hope I didn't include too many details about the setting, but I wanted readers to feel as if they were there.

In my opinion, the Yorkshire Dales are one of the most beautiful areas of England. The greenest fields, hundreds of sheep, the ancient stone walls, and the quaintest villages. Traveling is such an eye-opener.

If you liked this story, please consider leaving a review. Reviews are important to authors.

Sincerely,

Valerie Massey Goree

BIO:

Award winner Valerie Massey Goree resides in the beautiful Hill Country, northwest of San Antonio.

After serving as missionaries in her home country of Zimbabwe and raising two children, Valerie and her husband, Glenn, a native Texan, moved to Texas. She worked in the public school system for many years, focusing on students with special needs. Now retired, Valerie spends her time writing, traveling, and spoiling her grandchildren.

Valerie loves to hear from her readers.

Connect with Valerie:

- Check her website to learn more about her romantic suspense novels and Glenn's non-fiction books: valeriegoreeauthor.com
- You can sign up for her quarterly newsletter and email her from the website.
- Facebook Author Page. Valerie Goree, Author
https://www.facebook.com/profile.php?id=61561775916508

- GoodReads and BookBub
- Amazon Author Page
https://www.amazon.com/author/valeriegoreeauthor7523

Other Books By Valerie Massey Goree

Texas Suspense:
Deceive Me Once
Colors of Deceit

Stolen Lives Trilogy:
Weep in the Night
Day of Reckoning
Justice at Dawn

Stand Alone:
Forever Under Blue Skies

My Mother's Secret:
Shadows of Time
Every Hidden Thing

Series: From England with Love and…Treachery
Book 1: Meet Me Where the Windrush Flows

Series: Sister in Peril
Book 1: Dangerous Dalliance

Made in the USA
Monee, IL
13 February 2025